LAYING AUTUMN'S DUST

Mark L. Brooks

Co-Pilot Publishing LLC 2024

Laying Autumn's Dust:
A Southern Tragedy About Betrayal, Revenge, and Murder

First-time or interested authors, contact Co-Pilot Publishing at: Authorsassistance@copilotbooks.org
Or visit us at Copilotbooks.org

Edited by Ellen Zolkos

Cover Design by Matthew Clark

Author Photograph by Sydney Mae Photography, LLC

Printed on acid-free paper

Library of Congress Control Number: 2024940777

ISBN 979-8-9908542-1-5 (HC)
ISBN 979-8-9908542-0-8 (PB)

First Printing: June 2024

Dedicated to Minions of the Moon and absent friends—
There are many.

"So we beat on, boats against the current, borne back ceaselessly into the past."

-F. Scott Fitzgerald

CONTENTS

Prologue

Sheriff Castleberry smelled rotting flesh through his handkerchief. Pressing the cloth tighter against his mouth and bent nose, he eyed the crows cawing from the tie beam, then followed the rope down and studied the woman. Flies swarmed her swollen body. He nodded. "That's her." His voice was muffled. "Any signs of foul play?"

The deputy shook his head. "No scuffs in the dirt. Just her tracks. Best I can tell, she tied the rope to the crossbeam, took time to return the ladder, then jumped from the loft."

"You're assuming the boot prints belong to the boy who reported her?"

"They match."

The sheriff looked at the barn's collapsed roof. As he folded his handkerchief, he calculated the body was exposed to the August sun roughly three hours a day. "What do you reckon? A week?"

"At least." The deputy wiped his hands on his pants. "Why do it here? How long's it been since anyone lived in the house?"

"Ten, fifteen year."

"I be dog. Oh, I found these." He picked up two evidence bags and handed one to the sheriff.

Sheriff Castleberry removed the diary from the bag. He recognized the handwriting—and knew it didn't belong to the woman hanging from the beam. As he fanned through pages, something caught his eye, and he flipped back to the circled date. Then he read the part underlined in different ink. Feeling his pulse quicken, he looked at the deputy from beneath the brim of his hat. The deputy was waving his free hand at the crows. One hopped to a sagging rafter but didn't take flight. Holding his eyes on the deputy, Sheriff Castleberry slowly tore the page from the binding, slid the paper in his back pocket, and closed the diary.

Unable to intimidate the crows, the deputy turned. He squinted. "You okay?"

"How about that other one?" They exchanged bags, and the sheriff read the title of the second book through clear plastic, biting his lip. "What do you make of this one?"

"Search me. But it looks brand new. I'm betting she brung it, too."

"Maybe—or maybe it's the killer's signature." He laid the bag on the ground and adjusted his hat, the damp sweatband cool against his forehead. "I found the same book on the porch the day the owner died."

The deputy's mouth dropped open. "You think this is linked to the old murder case?"

"Revenge don't tell time."

"Who would take out revenge on her?"

"A madman." He stared at the corpse, his eyes flat. "That old moonshiner said it best: 'When the devil steals the angel's share, there'll be hell to pay'."

Book I

Jesse I

Savannah

She stood with her hand cupped above her eyes, staring toward the old silo in the field behind the filling station. I glanced at the silo, then looked at the girl again. Her shoulders was suntanned, and her sandy blonde hair hung to the middle of her back in a thick braid. She wore a red dress that come to her knees, and her legs looked smooth down to her sandals.

Two young boys was laughing and chasing each other in front of her. Dust kicked up as they planted their feet and changed directions. The shorter boy smacked the bigger one's arm and run to the girl, trying to keep her between them. They darted around her. She ignored them.

I watched her until she cut her eyes at me, then I shifted toward the gas pump. The numbers on the dial slowly rolled up. I wiped sweat off my brow.

"Ready for school to start?"

I turned my head. Mr. Sumner had stepped out of the car. He was smoking a cigar, his brimmed hat shading his face. He lived several miles down the road from my house and waved as he drove by, but about the only time we spoke was when I pumped his gas. He reared cattle, and sometimes when I helped Mr. Smith sling hay, we hauled a few loads to Mr. Sumner's barn and stacked the bales in the loft. His wife always brung us homemade lemonade after we was done. I'd drink it and listen to the men tell stories.

"Yes sir."

"What grade will you be in?"

"I'll be a senior."

He cocked his head like he hadn't heard at first. Then he said, "Lord 'a' mercy! I remember when you were no bigger than them". He nodded his chin toward the boys. They was sitting on their haunches now, poking a stick at something on the ground.

The handle clicked off. I pulled the nozzle from the tank and hung it on the pump, then held the license plate panel open while I tightened the gas cap. The panel snapped shut. Mr. Sumner hollered for the boys, and they bolted to the Cadillac. The older one stopped himself by slamming both hands on the hood, the other boy a few steps behind. They was sweating and breathing hard. Mr. Sumner gave them money for colas and told them to buy one for their sister, then he asked me to check the oil since they had a long drive ahead.

When I replaced the dipstick, the car rocked, and a door closed. I dropped the hood and seen the girl in the front seat. Then I washed the windshield, scrubbing splattered bugs off the glass. As I swiped it clean, I watched her from the corner of my eye. She was fingering her necklace. When she moved her hand aside, the pearl fell against her chest. She wasn't wearing no bra, and I seen her tan line and the whiteness of her small, rounded breasts. She kept her head down but raised her eyes and met mine, smiling. My stomach jumped, and I looked away.

As I washed the driver side, her brothers climbed in the car and gave her a Coke. Mr. Sumner paid me, and I walked to the garage and stood in the shade. The girl lifted the bottle to her lips, then cut her eyes at me again. I glanced down.

Grease and oil stains covered my shirt and blue jeans, and grime had caked around my fingernails from tinkering with engines. I thought about how clean and bright she had looked in the sun, then grabbed the rag hanging from my back pocket and wiped my hands, hoping she hadn't noticed my dirty nails. The service bell rung when the rear tires rolled over the hose, and I watched as they drove toward the freeway ramp, the heat shimmering on blacktop.

"Hey, Jesse," the owner said. "Did Mr. Sumner tip you?"

"Gave me a buck." Usually a dollar was a big deal. I had pumped gas at the filling station on weekends for a couple of years, and most folks didn't give nothing. I also done small repairs on cars, but the hard stuff went to Pop or Murry. Pop was the best mechanic in town and worked at Fred's during the week while I was at Billy Tucker's sawmill— at least in summertime.

I turned toward Fred. "Never seen that girl before."

He grinned. "That's Mr. Sumner's granddaughter from Savannah. Visits ever' summer."

I thought about her long hair, her blue eyes, and the curve of her tan shoulders. But what struck me most was her smile when she had caught me looking down her dress.

I walked to where them boys had been squatting on their heels. A dead lizard laid in the dirt. Its skin was still shiny, but I couldn't tell if they had been the ones who had killed it. The lizard's tail was gone, and its jaw was opened sideways, a speck of blood on its teeth. The flies I had spooked lit back on the body.

The sun hammered my neck, and my shirt was damp. When I straightened up, them flies scattered and buzzed again. Behind the silo, a tractor raked hay in rows for baling, and I wished Mr. Smith had cut the field a week earlier. I could've met the girl before she left town. Then I remembered a story Mr. Sumner had once told when we had took him hay—about how he had chased his daughter's boyfriend out of his barn with a shotgun. Mr. Smith had said it was a shame his son was never brave enough to sneak around with Mr. Sumner's daughter. Both men had laughed.

The service bell rung, and a rusted pickup stopped beside the pumps. I went and spoke to the driver. He had deep creases on his forehead, and his eyes was dark. He handed me a crumpled dollar bill and two dollars in coins. The change was heavy in my pocket. I pulled out the sock he used for a gas cap and draped it across the side of the truck bed. I slid the nozzle in the tank and squeezed the handle, then clicked it off at four dollars.

That night, in the light of the quarter moon, me and my buddy Evan sat on Number 9 bridge—where the railroad crossed Crawdad Creek—and I told him about Mr. Sumner's granddaughter. Evan claimed he would've winked at her through the windshield. He called her Savannah.

"Does this mean you've given up on Angie?"

I had carried a handful of railroad stones to the bridge and laid them on the crosstie beside me. "Piss off," I said, and tossed one at Evan. The stone hit his arm, and he laughed as it fell toward the creek.

Our freshman year, Angie Dobbins had split up with Monroe during homecoming week. Me and Evan had dressed for the varsity game, and on the sideline that Friday night, I had been more nervous about asking Angie for a dance than playing a few snaps against boys bigger than me. After the whistle had ended the game, I changed clothes in the fieldhouse and went to the gym and sat beside Evan. He danced with a couple of girls and even kissed one, but nobody had gone near Angie. By the last slow song, I had finally worked up my courage. Angie smiled when I asked her to dance. I put my hands on her waist, and she cupped my shoulders and laid her head on my chest. We swayed back and forth. As the song ended, she stared at me so long I almost broke a sweat, then I asked if she would go steady with me. She nodded.

When the bright lights come on, Angie looked toward the corner of the room, and I followed her eyes and seen Monroe watching. She took my hand as we walked out. On the walkway, she said her dad was waiting, so I let go of her hand. She stepped toward the parking lot, then turned. "Wanna go on a hayride?"

The next evening, about a dozen people sat in the wagon towed behind a tractor. The hay cushioned the bumps along the dirt road leading to Deerhead Cove Cemetery. Oak trees stretched black limbs over us, and when the wind blowed, dead leaves rattled in the branches. The graveyard wasn't far from my house, so I had walked through it before. Marble headstones lined the entrance, but in the back, rectangular rocks marked graves with names and dates almost wore off by weather. Them old tombstones was crooked from where the ground had settled.

Near the cemetery, I smelled woodsmoke and stood to look over the sideboard. Fires dotted a field. I knew loggers had burned brush piles from the land they had cleared, and I imagined greybacks huddled around them fires. Since it was close to Halloween, I figured everyone had seen ghosts through the smoky haze.

When we nestled beside each other again, Angie pulled the blanket to our necks. She leaned against me and rested her head on my shoulder, glancing up now and then. I knew she wanted me to kiss her.

After the hayride, me and Evan sat with our feet hanging from the railroad bridge. I bragged about putting my hand on Angie's knee under the blanket.

"You should've kissed her."

I told him I'd have plenty of chances for that. A scrap of paper with Angie's handwriting was in my pocket. I had already memorized her phone number.

Evan lit a cigarette. "She's a good kisser."

I jerked my head toward him. He said he had been at a birthday party and played a game where him and Angie had gone behind the house.

I stared at the creek, my heart beating faster. I could barely see the ripples on the surface in the dark. We didn't say nothing for a while. Evan flicked his cigarette butt, and the orange glow spun in circles until the water snuffed it.

On Monday morning, me and Evan stood at our lockers, and Angie's best friend come up and said Angie had broke up with me. She turned and hurried down the hall and stopped in front of Angie. Monroe leaned against the wall beside her. When he seen me, he smirked and bowed up. I fished Angie's number from my pocket and pinched the paper into a tiny wad and flung it on the floor. The homeroom bell rung, reminding me of a whistle ending a game I hadn't played in.

That afternoon, when I stepped off the school bus, the hood was raised on Mamma's car. Pop was laying beneath it with his legs stuck out, his boot heels just missing his beer when he shifted. Two other bottles laid beside it, and I knew he hadn't kicked them neither.

Jake barked, and I headed toward him. His chain went taut as he reared and pulled against it.

"Let 'im be, boy," Pop said. "Don't want 'im nosing around or spillin' nothin'."

When I turned, I seen another empty beer bottle off to the side. I walked to the car, put my books on the ground, and propped my hands on the fender. Pop tugged on something. The car shook. "Why ain't you at practice?"

I seen where Pop had cleaned part of the motor. "Got in a fight."

The car shook again, and Pop slid out from under it. He stood and dusted his pants, then took a swig and set the bottle on the roof. "Principal called. Told me what you done." He sniffed. "I was seein' if you'd lie to me." He held one hand in the other, running his thumb across his palm. Then he asked me what had happened.

When I was paddled at school, I got a whupping at home too—no matter the reason—and Pop had never cared to hear my side of the story. But he listened while I told him about the fight, and how several folks had to pull me off Monroe. I didn't tell him it was over a girl.

"Fought 'im to the ground, huh?"

"Yes sir." I remembered the tense silence as I had sat in the principal's office with Monroe. His lip was swolled up, and blood had stained his shirt from his busted nose. I had felt bad about ruining his shirt.

"He lay a good lick on you?"

"Yes sir. Couple." Monroe had landed a few punches, and my head still hurt, but I didn't have no mark to show for it.

Jake whimpered, and I heard his chain catch. My chest got tight.

Pop spat, then mixed the tobacco juice and dirt with the toe of his boot. When he looked up, he was smiling, and I seen pride in his crow's-feet. "Tough as nails," he said. He slapped me on the shoulder. My chest dropped, and I realized I had been holding my breath.

He finished his beer and rubbed his brow, leaving a black smudge. "Let's see if this bitch'll crank."

Pop scooted behind the steering wheel and left the door open, one foot on the ground. The engine fired, and he gunned it twice, then let it idle. A belt squealed. Pop frowned.

I walked to Jake and scratched behind his ears. He pawed at me, smearing dirt on my jeans. My head felt light, like when Monroe had clocked me, and I thought me and Pop had finally turned a corner.

The stone splashed in the creek, and my mind drifted from Pop and the fight back to the girl at the filling station. I remembered how she had moved her hand aside when I had cleaned the windshield. "At least I seen her titties. That's more than I done with Angie."

Evan held out his cigarette and tapped it. "Angie's got some good ones." I jerked my head toward him again. He laughed. "I had you there for a second."

A train horn blowed in the distance. We didn't budge until the headlight eased around the bend, then we hopped up and balanced on the railroad crossties, skipping from one to the other until the black emptiness between them become stone grey and we jumped off the tracks. The engine hummed.

We stood in the glow of the light, and the engineer blasted that horn from the bridge until he passed. The boxcars, tankers, and coal cars screeched and stirred up wind and dust as they rolled down the tracks. I seen Evan's mouth move, but the noise drowned him out. When the caboose went by, the steady beat faded, and we headed back to the bridge and dangled our legs off the edge. Evan dug his fingers in his shirt pocket for another cigarette and lit it. He tried to blow a smoke ring. "I'd like to ride a train."

Whenever we walked the tracks, Evan talked about how them coal cars would carry him down to Birmingham, where he could earn enough money in steel factories to live high on the hog. His daddy had told him them smokestacks was as tall as city skyscrapers.

We sat quiet while Evan smoked. A mist hovered above the creek and slowly spilled over the bank and crept into the woods, the way water done when it flooded. I heard the horn again, and I wondered how far away it was. Then I thought about seeing the heat rise from the asphalt on the empty road, the lizard in the dirt, and the girl. All day I had thought about the girl—her hand cupped above her eyes, her shining hair, her legs.

"She's comin' back next summer, ain't she?" Evan said, like he knew what I was thinking. "Gives you time to grow a pair." He looked at me sideways and grinned.

I throwed another stone. The mist swallered it, but I heard the kerplunk when it hit water. Mr. Sumner's story about chasing that boy off with a shotgun come to mind, and I knew, in his own way, Evan was right, and I wondered if I'd have the balls to sneak into Mr. Sumner's barn to meet his granddaughter.

Two weeks later, school started. Football practice was in full swing, and I was done with the sawmill for the year. Me and Evan sat beside each other in homeroom. A couple of pretty girls was in our class—but no one like Savannah.

Abigail I

My Night of Firsts

We kept a pistol in the nightstand on Donny's side of the bed. I made sure it was loaded and hurried to the porch. Tears burned my eyes, but I could see my husband clear enough to point the gun at him. I held the pistol steady with both hands and remembered how heavy it had felt the first time I had fired it.

Donny had wanted me to know how to handle a gun, so he had taken me shooting. We were just dating then, but we hoped to marry. Donny had parked beside a field and reached in the back of the truck for a couple of empty beer bottles and set them on opposite edges of a large stump. He showed me how to aim, warned about recoil, and helped me hit the first one. I was surprised at how loud the shot had sounded, but I smiled at Donny over my shoulder after the bottle shattered. Donny stepped aside and hooked his thumbs in the pockets of his old blue jeans. When I fired the pistol on my own, a dirt clod flew up in the field, then I chipped the stump, but on my third shot, I broke the other bottle.

Walking to the truck, I asked Donny where the bottles came from.

He sniffed. "I reckon they's Ricky's."

I looked sideways at him. "Do you always call him Ricky?"

Donny stopped. He spat tobacco juice in the dirt. "What else am I supposed to call 'im? He ain't my father. I sure as hell don't like him, and he sure as hell don't like me."

We stood quiet for a minute, Donny staring across the field. I wondered what was going through his mind, but he always put up a wall when I asked about his stepfather.

"What about the glass?" I said.

Donny was pressing his thumb in his palm. He seemed far away. "Do what?"

"Should we clean up the broken glass?"

"Ain't our problem." He headed to the truck.

I gathered the pieces anyway. When I placed them in the bed of the truck, I saw more bottles. And even though we went shooting a lot, we never ran out of targets.

The one time I knew where they came from was when the county fair was in town and Donny took me to the fairgrounds. We rode most of the rides and played some games. Donny liked the dunking tank, and he showed off his muscles by ringing the bell both times he swung the sledgehammer. When I saw the shooting gallery, I pulled Donny toward it by his sleeve.

I hit all the bullseyes, and the man at the booth told me to pick a prize. Then he said he would like to take me shooting.

Donny looked at the man. "Like hell you will."

"I didn't mean nothing by it," he said. "I just—"

Donny stretched across the counter and grabbed the man's collar with one hand and punched his face with the other. The man staggered, and I heard someone holler, "You can't let that slide—kick his ass, Donny!". Greg and Amy had walked up.

As I pulled Donny from the booth, I glanced back and saw the man holding his bloody nose. "You didn't have to hit him," I said, but I felt pride in the way my man had stood up for me.

Donny needed to simmer down, so the four of us went to his truck. He had hidden a cooler beneath blankets in the back, and he opened two beers and passed one to Greg. Amy smiled and took it from him, so Donny gave Greg another one and slid the bottle opener in his pocket. When Donny offered me his beer, I shook my head. I had never tried alcohol.

"Oh, c'mon, Abigail," Donny said. "One drink."

Greg and Amy watched. When I sipped it, they cheered. I held the beer toward Donny.

"You didn't even taste it," he said. "Take you a good pull." He winked at Amy, and she smiled again.

I took another sip. I knew what the preacher and my parents said about drinking, so the bottle felt heavy. Donny waved off the beer, opened one for himself, and chugged it. He set his empty bottle in the bed of the truck and popped another cap, and I thought about all the targets I had shattered. "You said those bottles were Ricky's."

"They was." He grinned. "But the beer was mine."

They all laughed, but I wondered what other lies Donny had told.

"Y'all best shove off if you're gonna drink," a voice said. "Maybe try Groper's Grove."

When I turned and saw the deputy, I hid the beer behind my back. I recognized him, but I couldn't remember his name. He had graduated a couple of years ahead of me.

"Didn't figure you for a drinker, Abby," he said.

Greg smiled like he knew something we didn't. "We were just leaving, sir."

"We never had this conversation." The deputy strolled away.

"Good Lord, Donny, what have you gotten me into? He'll tell my father, sure as the world."

"Don't worry about him," Greg said. "That's my cousin. He'd join us if he wasn't on duty."

Greg said he would get his car later, so we piled in the cab of Donny's truck and cruised around. After a while, we drove down a dirt road leading to a field where several other vehicles were parked. A few of them looked familiar. The headlights were off, and I could see the grove in the soft moonlight. Although I had never been there, I knew where we were. People called it different names, but they all meant the same thing.

"You want the front or back?" Donny said.

Amy giggled.

"The closer to the beer, the better," Greg said, and he and Amy climbed in the truck bed. He handed Donny two beers, and Donny rolled up his window and pulled me next to him.

"What if someone sees?"

Donny grunted. "Ain't nobody lookin'." He took a drink. "Besides, none of us is even here." I didn't know what he meant. I sipped the beer, then put the bottle between my legs.

"Oh, c'mon, Abigail."

"We agreed to wait until we're married."

Donny stared straight ahead. "Well, we should wait, then."

But it wasn't like other times we had talked about waiting. Everyone had come to the grove for the same reason, and I glanced through the rear window and saw Greg and Amy moving under the blankets.

I learned what Donny had meant about none of us being there, and it seemed like I had joined a secret club. But some secrets had a way of revealing themselves, only giving hints at first, like a few empty beer bottles in the back of a truck.

I buttoned my blouse and looked out the window. The moon had shifted behind a tree's canopy, and the leaves were black against its glow. All the other vehicles were gone, and Greg and Amy were asleep. I wondered what time it was. Then I noticed headlights crawling along the lane lined with trees. The car came into the clearing, but unlike other cars that had given us a wide berth, this one moved toward the truck and stopped, keeping a gap between us. The car's engine revved. I put my hand on Donny's thigh and squeezed.

Donny rolled down his window and stuck out his head. "Cut your lights off!"

Greg rose, shading his eyes, and someone yelled Donny's name.

I grabbed Donny's arm. "What's going on?"

"It's nothin'."

Donny stepped out, leaving his door open. A man spoke to him, but I couldn't hear what he said. I saw two more figures silhouetted against the car's lights. My hands started shaking.

Donny raised his voice. "Let's do this later, fellers. I'm with my gal."

"We're doing it now," a man said.

"What the hell do you want?" Greg shouted. Amy sprang up.

"This don't concern you," the man said, pointing at Greg.

"The hell it don't!" He leaped from the truck.

All at once, Greg was on the ground, and two men were fighting Donny. Amy screamed and climbed out of the truck and ran to Greg, hitting the man who had him pinned. A man swung something at Donny, and he covered his ribs and dropped to one knee. Then I remembered the gun. My hands still shook, but I snatched the pistol from the glovebox and opened the passenger door. I fired in the air, then rested my wrists on the bedside of the truck to hold steady.

The men eased from Donny, who was laying on his back. Amy was kneeling over Greg. I kept the gun aimed at the men. I heard doors shut and saw the headlights backing away. The car spun around and sped down the lane. I almost fainted.

I tossed the pistol on the seat and hurried to Donny. He was propped on one elbow, wiping his mouth. Greg and Amy came over, and I asked Donny who the men were. He said they must have been friends with the man from the shooting gallery, but that didn't make sense to me, and it seemed like I had found another empty beer bottle.

I wrapped my arm around Donny's waist and walked him to the truck. He leaned against the edge of the seat in the cab's light. His lip was cut, and he winced when he felt his ribs.

"How'd they know we were here?" I said.

"Sorry I wasn't more help," Greg said. He gave Donny a beer. "They whupped us good."

"Weren't no fair fight." Donny spat blood on the ground. "I appreciate you jumpin' in."

"Sharpshooter is the one you should thank," Greg said. "Didn't know you had a gun. Boy, they sure lit out!"

Donny put his hand on my shoulder and smiled.

I was still shaken up when Donny drove me home. Father was awake and caught me sneaking in the house and smelled beer on my breath. It was our first awkward situation of me breaking the rules and Father deciding how to punish me. But even though he grounded me on the spot, I was more concerned about what had happened with Donny. Something was off. So I laid in bed and stared in the dark, tracing events from the fairgrounds to the grove and recalling the conversations between Donny, Greg, and Amy. I wondered—if I had kept a diary like Amy, and knowing the world was full of idle hands and prying eyes—what I would have been willing to write. Since I was so preoccupied with fights, shooting the pistol, and suspicion, I didn't have time to feel guilt for losing my virginity in the cab of Donny's truck in a field called Groper's Grove.

My night of firsts finally wore me down, and as I drifted to sleep, it dawned on me—I never got my prize.

Sometime later, I learned a few details, shedding more light on that night, and between Donny's gambling debt and the secret he and I shared, we would never be the same. But I handled the changes better than Donny, and only a hint of our secret showed on our wedding day.

So when I took the gun from the nightstand and went to the porch, thinking about the first time I had fired it, my eyes burned, and tears streamed down my face. Our lives had become such a mess I didn't know if I would ever be able to patch them up, but I was tired of being scared, and I knew it was time to take a stand.

I aimed over Donny and remembered a passage from Isaiah: *There shalt be heaviness and sorrow, and thou shalt be brought down and thy speech shall whisper out of the dust.*

I squeezed the trigger. The hammer hit its breaking point and slammed closed. The recoil threw my hands up and back, and the shot tore through the night.

Donny whipped his head toward me. For the first time in my life, he was waiting for me to tell him what to do.

"Get off my son." The dust he and Jesse had stirred up as they had fought hovered over them. "Get off him, or I'll kill you." I held the gun steady.

Donny stood, not taking his eyes from me. Blood was smeared on his shirt. I didn't know if it was his or Jesse's. The dog started barking.

"You ever lay a hand on either of us," I said, "I'll kill you."

He looked at Jesse and back at me. He stepped forward, and I heard the click as I cocked the hammer. He stopped and glared at me, then spat. "You c'n all go to hell."

My heart raced, and my throat knotted. Donny turned and walked toward the shed, out from the glow of the porch light. I eased pressure off the trigger but kept the gun on him until his silhouette blended with darkness. I almost fainted.

Donny I

Warning Shot

I didn't look back as I walked to the shed in the dark, but I could feel the gun tracking me. Abigail weren't no killer, but she'd've shot me dead if I had took another step toward her. I run my tongue over my lip and tasted blood. They can all go to hell, I thought.

I pulled the string hanging from the bare light bulb, then worked the axe back and forth from the V that had been cut in the edge of the chopping block. I set up a piece of firewood and brung down the blade. Both halves kicked up dust where they landed. I balanced one on end and split it again. After stacking the wood, I found a piece full of knots. The blade stuck on the first swing, but the log cracked, so I jammed a wedge in the crease and swung the sledgehammer. The metal rung with each stroke. I freed the axe and finished splitting the log, then put more wood on the block.

I scratched my whiskers. When I had taught Abigail to shoot, I had never figured I'd be on the business end of the barrel. It was a hell of a thing to be shot at with your own gun.

The warning shot had reminded me of the other time she had fired the gun in the air. She had showed a lot of grit in Groper's Grove. She had drunk beer, we had screwed in my truck, and she had held a gun on them boys who had hit me with the baseball bat. I could've fell in love with a girl like that.

But Abigail weren't the only one who had fooled me that night. I had also been proud of Greg for jumping in the fight—until I heard him and his cousin had betrayed me. Somehow Greg had caught wind me and Amy was seeing each other behind his back, so he had sold me out to them boys to settle the score. When I learnt that, I prob'ly would've killt Greg at the poolhall had our buddies not pulled me off of him.

I figured Amy weren't involved with the setup since we had knocked boots after the night in the grove, but when I beat hell out of Greg, she was so mad at me she had tried to end it. When I explained what had happened, she said she needed time to think, but at that point, I didn't realize I was the one short on time.

Onc't the dust settled, I knowed I had played my cards wrong. Thumping Greg had put me on the bad side of the law, and Amy had cut me off. Abigail stopped drinking, and she only spread her legs when she was in the mood. And she weren't never in the mood after she learnt about me and Amy.

"My gut told me something was going on between you two," Abigail had said, standing in my kitchen.

It weren't worth denying, so I crossed my arms and propped against the counter. I was done with Abigail. We had the house to ourselves, and I had tried to kiss her when she first come over, but she had pushed me away. All she wanted to do was talk about getting married, so I decided to let her speak her mind before I broke up with her.

"Mother was right about you. She told me not to get mixed up with a Hartline."

"What the hell does that mean?"

"Figure it out, Donny! You drink too much, you gamble too much, you fight too much, and from the sound of it, you—"

She stopped. Tears filled her eyes and run down her cheeks.

"If I'm so bad, why don't you leave me?"

She was sobbing now, and her shoulders was shaking. She put her face in her hands.

"Is that what you want?"

She mumbled through sobs.

I grabbed her arms so hard she had bruises the next day. "Look at me when I'm talkin' to you!"

Her head snapped up, and she was on fire. "Yes," she screamed, "that's what I want!" She spat in my face.

I didn't realize what I done until I seen her crumpled on the floor.

I wiped her spit on my sleeve and rubbed the back of my hand where her teeth had cut it. "You sure got grit," I said, standing over her. "I'll give you that."

She raised up and leaned against the cabinet door. Her eyes met mine again, but this time she seemed wore out. "I can't leave you," she said. "I want to. But I can't."

"Because you love me too much." I was fixing to tell her it was over, and I imagined her surprise.

"This isn't love, Donny. It's life. I'm pregnant."

My stomach felt similar to when that bat had busted my ribs. I didn't know what to do, so I slid down beside her. After a minute, I said, "You gonna keep it?".

Her glare could've bore a hole through me. And what she said next near did. "*We*, Donny. *We* are keeping *our* baby." Then she started crying again.

My heart had jumped in my throat as I realized my future was set in stone. I was suddenly exhausted, and I pulled Abigail close and held her in my arms. "It'll be alright," I said, but it sounded like a lie. She buried her face in my chest, her tears soaking through my shirt. Her body was hot against me. "Everything will be alright," I said again, and I kissed the top of her head. She clutched my shirt tighter.

Now, in the shed, standing in the light of the naked bulb, I remembered our short engagement, and how Abigail had a slight bump in her white dress when we had married, and how that day had seemed like any other day—and I wondered if I would've felt different if it hadn't been no shotgun wedding.

I was splitting the last log, pumping the axe handle, and the blade squeaked free. I set the wedge and swung the sledgehammer, the wood cracking as the wedge ripped it apart. The log twisted and fell from the chopping block, and the wedge hit the ground with a thud. Long splinters barely held the two halves together. I picked up the axe and propped the handle against my thigh, the toe of the blade in the dirt. I smelt fresh oak and noticed shades of red and brown in the heart of the wood. Gripping the knob, I leaned on the axe and thought about the sound of the bullet slicing the air. I looked where Abigail had stood aiming my gun steady—the way I had taught her. The porch light was still on, and I seen the head of the broken broom laying in the yard. I run my hand over my whiskers again. If I was her, I thought, I wouldn't've fired no warning shot.

Jesse II

Crow's-Feet

Once the season started, football was on my mind more than Savannah. Them hot, August practices drained me, and I looked forward to autumn when I wouldn't be wringing sweat from my socks. But all the heat, hard hits, and pain was worthwhile when I laid a good lick on somebody.

Pop had taught me how to wrap people up, and I was the best tackler on the team. When I was younger, playing football with Pop in the yard had been fun. We would pass the ball, practice trick plays, and tackle each other. At first, I knew he let me drag him to the ground. But he would only fall when I used good form. If I ducked my head or hit him too high, he would slough me off.

I had made varsity my sophomore year, and after that season opener, Pop had told me to stay outside when we had got home.

"You played good tonight," he had said, "but you could've done better." He had rattled off the total yards and points I had allowed by missing four tackles. I had reminded him of the score, and he had said winning by three touchdowns wasn't no excuse for sloppiness. He had fastened Jake to his chain and marked a scrimmage line on the ground with a stick, then broke down in a three-point stance. He had rushed at me and laid me flat. Extending his arm, he had pulled me to my feet and explained what I done wrong. By the third tackle, though, he had stopped helping me up. When I had finally brung him down four times, he had stood, dusted off, and walked toward the porch, leaving me laying in the dirt. "If you're a man, you'll get up," he had said over his shoulder. The screen door had smacked the frame twice when he had stepped in the house. That sound become my signal to relax.

Before long, I had realized Pop plowing over me wasn't about helping me—it was something he done for himself, reliving his schooldays. But as much as I dreaded going home after rough games, Pop improved my tackling.

By the fifth game my senior year, the temperature had cooled, and the wind usually blowed in the evenings. On the Friday Stevenson come to town, we was 2-2, but they was undefeated and had their sights set on another state championship. Stevenson was the only team in our area with black players. When their running back first carried the ball, a couple of my teammates yelled stuff at him. The referees gave us a warning, so Coach put a stop to it. Them boys must've been used to it, playing the likes of us each week, and they never mouthed off. They just kept laying the wood to us.

The running back's name was Rogers. He was one of the best in the state and run around or through me more times than I could count—but I knew Pop was keeping track.

We was losing by a bunch at halftime, and Coach tried to motivate us with his "Character, Grit, Never Quit" speech. But as I glanced around the fieldhouse, I seen the same look on everybody's face, and I thought Pop's saying would've struck a better chord: It ain't how bad you get thumped, but how fast you get back on your feet.

Stevenson never took their foot off the gas, but late in the game, I finally planted a square hit on Rogers, and he fumbled. While we laid on the field with our facemasks touching, Rogers looked me dead in the eye.

"Good lick."

My stomach jumped. I squinted and gave a nod. Teammates hauled me up, slapping my helmet. Rogers trotted to the sideline, then doubled over with his hands on his knees.

Stevenson kneeled on the ball to end the game, and I stepped up to Rogers.

"Good game."

He gave a quick nod, and then his teammates pulled him away, swatting his helmet. I knew how that part felt, but I didn't know the glory behind it. All I done was make one play, and I had been embarrassed when my teammates had danced around me.

After the game, Mamma said losing to an undefeated team was nothing to be ashamed of and she was proud of me. Pop stayed quiet. The ride home was long. I rested my forehead on the cool window and stared into the darkness, hoping Evan could rustle up some of his daddy's beer for our night on the bridge.

When Pop parked the car in the drive, Mamma put her hand on his sleeve. "They've won every game, Donny."

"Get on in the house."

As Mamma went inside, I stood next to Jake. He sat, panting. Pop dug his thumb in his palm, then crossed his arms and slouched against the hood of the car. He cocked his head. I looked down, my shoulder throbbing from all my attempts to tackle Rogers. I needed to ice it.

Pop sniffed. "I seen you talkin' to that nigger." He spat on the ground, and the tobacco juice splattered. "I seen 'im run away from you. What'd you tell 'im?"

I now knew why Pop hadn't marked a scrimmage line. I also knew what he wanted to hear. Mamma had told me never to use that word, but my shoulder couldn't take no more hits, so I figured I'd just say it and be done.

"I called him a nigger."

Pop swiped his foot, mixing his spit with dirt, and I looked up. He would've thumped me good if I had said anything else. I wasn't so sure he wasn't going to thump me then—until he smiled. He smiled and nodded, and them crow's-feet latched on. Them claws seemed to dig in deeper every day, and I wondered how long it would take before they squeezed all the life from Pop's eyes.

Pop put his hand on my shoulder and tightened his grip, but not enough to hurt. "You done good, boy." He strode past, and I heard his boots tap each porch step. The screen door smacked twice.

I laid down, and Jake nuzzled me. His nose was wet. Low, dark clouds streaked across the sky, and when they hid the moon, their shifting edges glowed. I run my fingers in

Jake's fur and thought about what I had told Pop, and how my legs had felt weak when I had said it—but not because I lied.

A few weeks later, I played the worst game of my life. My body was tired, I was sore, and my shoulder still hurt. But I was mainly distracted. It was our first game without Evan. The offense couldn't get no traction without his speed, so our defense hardly left the field. By the fourth quarter, we gave up ten yards a carry. Our goal-line stands and their bad kicker was all that saved us from being blowed out.

When the game ended, I jogged to the fieldhouse with the team. I pulled off my cleats and turned them upside down—something I done after I had a bad game, something only Evan knew.

I sat with my shoulder pads and helmet hanging behind me. Evan's empty locker was next to mine. His last name and jersey number was scribbled on a strip of athletic tape above his bare hooks on the wall. I propped my forearms on my thighs and stared at a jagged crack in the concrete floor. Coach walked by and clapped me on the back. "Keep your head up, Hartline."

During the game, teammates had made comments about missing Evan on offense, but as I looked at the crack, I knew that was only part of it for me. At first, I had been mad at Evan for not letting me know he was leaving, then I had realized he had been telling me for a long time. He had wrote a letter to his parents, and his mom had asked me if he had ever mentioned running away. I had pretended not to know nothing. Evan's note hadn't said where he went, but I had imagined him climbing the ladder of a metal car, sitting on a pile of coal, and riding a southbound train.

"Let's go, boy."

That voice made the train disappear. Pop was leaning against the doorway. The fieldhouse was empty, but I heard Coach on the phone in the office. I gripped the straps of my bag and slipped past Pop. His eyes was bloodshot.

He staggered to the parking lot, but he wouldn't let Mamma drive. When we was on the dirt road, she grabbed the wheel as he veered toward the ditch.

"Good Lord, Donny! You're going to kill us!"

Pop laughed.

At home, when he shut off the ignition, the keys dropped in the floorboard, and he groped for them in the dark.

"Go inside, Jesse. I need to speak to your father."

"Like hell you do," Pop said. He reached across her and fumbled for the handle and flung the door open. Her foot hooked the side panel when he shoved her, and she landed on her elbow. He throwed the keys at her.

I hopped out and helped her stand.

She leaned close. "Come inside. He scares me when he's all liquored up."

"I'll be fine. He's seein' double."

Mamma kissed my forehead, found the keys, and went toward the house. I called Jake and clipped the chain to his collar, then turned and seen Pop in the yard. He swayed, and I knew I'd run over him as many times as he wanted.

We stood toe-to-toe.

"Lost count of your missed tackles by halftime."

I smiled when he slurred.

Next thing I knew I was on the ground. Pop was between me and the porch light, his silhouette towering over me. "So you just need your ass whupped."

He reared back his foot, but I scrambled out of the way. I regained my feet, still dazed from his sucker punch. He took a jab and lost his balance. I swung, and my blow glanced off his head, then his uppercut jacked my jaw, and I was on the ground again.

"Ain't like fightin' that pansy at school, huh?"

Mamma yelled at Pop from the porch. Jake raised Cain.

"Come on, boy!" he said, and his boot caught me in the gut. I dodged the next kick, then seen Mamma whack his back with her broom. The wood snapped, and Pop stumbled forward. Then he turned toward Mamma. He snatched the broken handle from her and struck her across the temple. She fell.

I jumped up and rammed my good shoulder into his side. We both went down, and he swung them fists like hammers.

Pop was right. It was different from when I had fought Monroe. At school, people had gathered and cheered, ready to break it up if the fight got out of hand. But now my only chance was to get to Jake.

I pushed away, and we stood, facing each other. He missed with another jab, but he grazed my cheek with a right hook. I rolled with it, then lunged with all my weight behind my punch and nailed him square on his nose. His head jerked sideways. When he brung it around, blood poured over his lips and chin. He seemed sober all of a sudden and grinned. I seen red on his teeth. He sprung forward. I snagged his collar as I tripped backwards, and we fell, then he shuffled to his knees, straddling me. He clutched my shirt with one hand and drawed back his fist.

A shot rung out.

Jake quit barking, and Pop froze, his fist raised. Dust hovered, catching light from the porch.

"Get off my son."

Mamma was holding the pistol. Her voice shook, but me and Pop both knew she could handle a gun. Jake tugged at his chain and started barking again, and other dogs howled deep in the hollow.

"Get off him, or I'll kill you."

Pop wasn't grinning no more.

I had never seen Pop afraid of nothing, but I could tell he wasn't sure what Mamma would do. He slid off, moving slow and keeping his eyes on her. Mamma held the gun steady.

Pop's chin and the top of his shirt was red. He looked at each of us in turn, even Jake. "You c'n all go to hell." He spat blood and strode toward the shed. Mamma drawed a bead on him until he melted in the shadows.

Abigail II

Reasons He Would Never Know

I laid on Donny's kitchen floor thinking Mother was right, and I remembered what she had said. If I took her advice, all I had to do was stand and walk away, and Donny would be out of my life. I had just spat on Donny and told him I wanted to leave him, and now I wished it were that simple.

After Mother had learned I was pregnant, she had used my baby against Donny and said he would be a deadbeat parent, and she had insisted I end the relationship. Then she had shared her plan.

"I can't do it," I had said.

"I didn't say, 'Do it', Abby. Just consider it, rather than throw away your life with that trash." Her voice sounded hateful, and her upper lip curled.

"Please don't call him that. Donny's the father of my child."

"He doesn't have to be."

"Good Lord, Mother, is that what you did with me?"

"Don't sass me, young lady! Your father and I did things properly. We didn't gallivant in cow pastures before we married."

I thought about telling her we hadn't been in a pasture, but I knew it wouldn't make a difference. Instead, I said, "Does the preacher know your idea?" I hoped to shut her up, but she didn't miss a beat.

"I grant he'd rather you marry a good Christian boy like Jefferey Smith. He sure lights up when you're around."

Ever since I had been old enough to date, Mother had pushed me toward Jefferey. "How many times have I told you? I'm not interested in Jefferey Smith!"

Mother slapped her palm on the table, causing me to jump. "We are beyond the point of your interests!" She adjusted her bracelet. "What matters now is your child."

I leaned forward, poking my finger against my chest. "That's right—*my* child!"

She sighed. "Do you honestly believe a drunk grease monkey can feed three mouths?"

"They're called mechanics." I had already worried about Donny's wages—especially since I would need to quit the diner when my baby was born—but I would never admit that fact to Mother, so I reminded her Donny had repaired her car a few weeks ago.

"I was shocked he had the decency to show up sober. Jefferey Smith doesn't drink—I promise you that." She propped her elbow on the table and put her forehead on her hand, shaking her head. "Sweet Jesus, what will people think?"

"Let me get this straight. You want me to visit Jefferey and just sleep with him?"

"Heavens no!" she said, looking up. "Don't be vulgar. Bat your eyes and smile at him on Sunday. Then do that thing where you laugh and touch his arm, and I guarantee he'll ask you on a date." She laced her fingers together. "He's shy, so the rest is up to you."

"Do you hear yourself? You sound crazy!" I stood and snatched the car keys and slammed the door on the way out. I rolled down the window and drove. The crisp wind tangled my hair.

After a while, I found myself on the lane where Donny and I had first made love. We had been romantic several times since that night, and it had become harder for me to stand my ground—not just because Donny would get irritated, but because I enjoyed the closeness. "C'mon, Abigail," he would say. "We already done it. What's the big deal?" But it was a big deal to me, and I always felt guilt afterwards since we weren't married.

I gazed at the trees across the field and noticed the leaves had begun turning colors, and I considered how different my life would be next autumn. I placed my hand on my stomach. Donny was the only man I had ever loved, but as I had learned more about him, I had grown afraid of that love. I knew Mother had always feared it too. But she didn't know Donny the way I did. She never saw his tender moments—he held my hand and rubbed my leg at the movies, and he stroked my hair when we cuddled on the swing; he made me laugh, and it was exciting to be with him when we shot guns or cruised through town or went to the poolhall—and she had never heard him brag about me to his friends.

Still, I wasn't blind to his rough side, and those empty beer bottles kept stacking up. But most of Donny's faults could be improved or forgiven, and we would both need to make changes in our lives once we had a baby.

When I saw Father later that day, I knew by how he looked away from me Mother had already told him. I wasn't sure if she did it to protect me from his initial reaction or because she couldn't keep a secret, but they were both at the kitchen table when I returned. I sat in a chair with my hands in my lap and waited. I noticed a pattern shaped like an eye in the table's woodgrain.

Mother cleared her throat, and when I glanced up, Father lowered his eyes.

"Abby," Mother finally said, "Your father and I—"

The front door opened and closed, and my sister barged in holding her schoolbooks. She stopped in the doorway to the kitchen when the three of us turned toward her and stared.

"What's going on?" Jackie said.

"Go play in your room, Pumpkin," Mother said.

"Did Abby get caught drinking again?"

"We'll discuss it later," Mother said.

"But—"

"Go to your room, Jackie," Father said, flashing her a look. She stomped out.

Jackie had helped break the ice for Father. Our eyes met, and I saw his disappointment. I had only prepared for his anger. I shifted. The wooden seat creaked.

"Well," he said, "whatever you decide, you'd best make it quick. I suspect this Jefferey boy can count." His chair squeaked on the floor as he slid from the table. When he walked outside, Mother stepped to the window, arms crossed.

"That's the first he's spoken about it," she said, her back still toward me. She left the room.

I called Donny and told him we needed to see each other and to be thinking about anything he should tell me, and as I drove to his house, I made a mental list of everything I wanted to say.

He was on the porch when I arrived. He set his beer on the rail and kissed me, then led me inside. We kissed again, and he wanted more, but I brushed his hands from me.

"Oh, c'mon, Abigail."

"Don't give me that. We need to talk."

"We c'n talk anytime," he said, but I pushed him away again. He leaned back, gripping the edge of the countertop. "Fine," he said. "Talk."

"I love you, but if we marry, we should be on the same page." The other times we had discussed marriage, the wedding had always been down the road—not right around the corner—and maybe he had been telling me what he assumed I wanted to hear. So I explained how church and family were important to me, and we talked about his drinking and fighting. Then I added I wouldn't tolerate his betting. "So promise you won't gamble anymore."

"Can't afford to gamble no more." He smirked.

"It's not funny. Promise."

"A'ight then. I promise."

I bit my lower lip before asking him the question he had probably been dreading. "Are the rumors true?"

He played dumb.

"Is it true about you and Amy? Is that why you broke Greg's nose?"

"You know why I broke his nose."

"And Amy?"

His eyes narrowed when I said her name again. He stood up straight. "What of her?"

My stomach turned, like it had done earlier that morning. "Good Lord, Donny! We're going steady!"

He sniffed. "Well, it ain't steady enough."

I gritted my teeth, picturing them together, wondering if it had been the whole time we had dated. "My gut told me something was going on between you two."

He tried to pull me toward him, but I punched his chest with the bottom of my fists and pushed. He folded his arms and tilted his head to one side.

"Mother was right about you." My throat knotted. I recalled the looks Donny had given Amy—the winks, the smiles—and even though he had said he loved me plenty of times, I no longer believed it was true. Suddenly, Mother's idea didn't sound so crazy, and I told Donny I wanted to leave him. He grabbed and shook me. With my arms pinned, all I could do was spit in his face.

Donny had never struck me before, and I was so mad it didn't even hurt. But I knew I would feel it later.

So as I laid on the floor with Donny glaring down at me, those tender moments flickered in my mind and vanished. I felt drained. Donny had lied to me, cheated on me, and now he had hit me. But if I stayed quiet, it was over. "You're not lying if you don't say anything," Mother had said.

I touched my lip and looked at the blood on my fingertips. Just stand and walk out, I thought.

But the more I considered living a lie for the rest of my life and the consequences if Jefferey or my child learned the truth, the more I realized I couldn't walk away.

Heart heavy and legs weak, I sat up and stared at Donny. "I can't leave you," I said. Then I told him I was pregnant. All at once, his anger was gone, and I saw surprise on his face, then it went blank. He sunk down beside me and held me in his arms. I needed someone at that moment, and he was all I had, so I rested my head on his chest and cried. I cried for reasons he would never know.

Donny II
Buckshot

Grasshoppers jumped and buzzed over the fresh hay as I stared across the field. No, I thought, I sure as hell don't like Ricky.

I had just showed Abigail how to shoot a gun. I had helped her hit one bottle, then stood off to the side and made her break the second one on her own. She had flinched when she had pulled the trigger. The bottle had sat on a stump, and the slug plowed a furrow behind it.

"Might try holdin' the gun steady."

She had flashed a dirty look at me—but she smiled. On her second shot, the bullet took a chunk from the edge of the stump.

"Might try keepin' your eyes open."

She had swung that pistol toward me. "Might try keeping your mouth shut!"

I hadn't hit the ground that fast and that hard since I had played football. She had doubled over, the gun dangling at her side.

"Goddammit," I had said, standing. "Don't never point a gun at nobody unless you aim to use it." She had kept laughing. "It ain't funny, Abigail," I had said, but she got me tickled, and I had started laughing too. I had dusted off my britches.

She had straightened up, aimed, and fired. When the bottle shattered, she had blowed the tip of the barrel, like she was some hotshot. She had looked at me sideways and smiled, and I had walked up and kissed her. I had took the gun and tucked it in my waistband. She had hugged me, and we had kissed again and held hands as we headed to the truck. Then she had ruint it by asking about Ricky.

Abigail was always nosing around my business with my stepfather and asking why I never mentioned him or why I called him Ricky. It weren't no secret, but the more she pried, the more it bothered me, so I never said nothing. This time it was my fault for saying his name, but I couldn't think of no other excuse fast enough to explain them beer bottles in the bed of my truck, and Abigail didn't know Ricky left most of his empties near road signs.

I had let go of her hand and turned toward the field.

Ricky was a good-sized drinker, but I had plenty of other reasons for not liking him. He was bossy, he never took me hunting or fishing, and he only wanted me around when he needed something. But the main reason I hated him was because he had made me do his dirty work at Mr. Buffington's liquor store—then betrayed me.

The first time I stolt for him I was ten. Ricky had made it clear I didn't have no say in the matter. So when he parked the truck, I had followed him through the heavy glass door.

Bottles—different shapes and sizes—had lined the shelves. Ricky had picked one up, set it back on the shelf, and eased along another aisle. Whenever he touched something, I gauged if I could hide it under my shirt. He had told me to keep my eyes down, but I couldn't help but glance at the man standing behind the counter. Onc't he was watching me, but usually he was reading the newspaper. He wore his eyeglasses on the tip of his nose, and his cigarette moved with his lips as he read.

As we neared the back, Ricky turned a bottle of whiskey in his hand. I recognized the brand from our kitchen cabinet. This time he placed it on the bottom shelf.

"Tie your shoe, son." Ricky lit a cigarette as he headed toward the cooler.

I dropped to one knee and pretended to tie my shoelace. My hands tremored.

"Can't smoke in here," the man said.

When I heard his voice, I slid the bottle from the shelf and stuffed it halfway in my pants, my belt holding it snug against me.

"Do what?" Ricky said.

I pulled my shirttail down and stood. My nerves was shot.

"No smoking in the store," the man said.

"You gotta be shittin' me."

"My store. Don't like it, there's the door." He stared at Ricky over his glasses and through his own cigarette smoke.

Ricky stepped out, and for a blink, I feared he had stranded me. But before the door closed, he come back and walked to the cooler. He snagged a six-pack. When he paid,

I stood so close I smelt smoke on his shirt. I didn't look at the man. Ricky shoved the coins in his pocket, and we left. He got his cigarette off the icebox while I climbed in the truck.

"Give it," he said, as we pulled from the parking lot. He seen me shaking when I handed him the bottle.

He grinned at the whiskey and set it on the seat between us, then flipped his cigarette butt out the window. "Toss me one of them beers." He popped off the cap and put the bottle opener on the dashboard and held the beer toward me. "You earned it."

I hesitated.

"Go on, 'fore I change my mind."

I took the beer and tasted it, trying to keep a straight face.

"Ain't nobody likes it the first time." He rested his wrist on top of the steering wheel. "They say it's an *acquired* taste. Take you another sup."

It weren't no good the second time neither. I wiped my mouth with the back of my hand.

He laughed and reached for the beer. When he finished, he held the empty bottle by the neck, stretching his arm out the window. Then he flung it over the cab of the truck. It clanged against the stop sign. Ricky never slowed.

Over the next two years, we went to the liquor store whenever the hard stuff run low. After a while, Ricky and Mr. Buffington knowed each other by name. Ricky always bought beer, and now and again, he ponied up for whiskey to appear honest, but our routine didn't fluctuate. The only difference was the amount of shaking and sipping I done swopped places. But even though drinking helped afterwards, I never took a shine to pilfering.

Ricky had a good thing going until we got caught and he was banned. I was almost out the door one day when Mr. Buffington grabbed my jacket collar and yanked me back, and the bottle fell and busted.

About the time I heard it shatter and seen them pieces of glass sliding across the floor like ice cubes, Ricky backhanded me so hard he knocked me down. A chunk of glass lodged in my palm when I landed, and my nose almost touched the floor. The cut from the glass and sting from the alcohol brung tears to my eyes. The whiskey smelt strong.

"Boy, what would your maw say?" Ricky said. "You're gonna work off ever' cent of that bottle." He turned to Mr. Buffington. "He'll work off ever' cent." He jerked me up.

Blood covered my palm, and it burnt like hell. I couldn't fight back the tears. Some of them was from the pain in my hand.

Mr. Buffington had removed his glasses and was staring Ricky down, and Ricky lost that battle when he spun toward me. "Serves you right," he said. "We ain't thieves." He found the gumption to look at Mr. Buffington again. "I'll pick him up at close." He walked to the truck with his beer cradled in his arm and drove away.

I stood in the puddle of whiskey and broken glass, my jacket hanging on my elbows, still holding my hurt hand, bleeding and crying.

Under his breath, Mr. Buffington said, "Goddammit," and shook his head. He took me by the arm, gently, and led me to the sink in the bathroom. He turned on the cold water and gripped my wrist. I clinched my teeth and sucked in air as he worked the piece free. The glass clattered in the sink when he dropped it. Through the blur, I watched the water thin my blood as it swirled down the drain.

"The bad news," Mr. Buffington said, "is you got yourself one hell of a slice. The good news is it won't get infected with all that alcohol." He stepped out.

I held my palm beneath the faucet, then cupped water in my other hand and splashed my face. With the bathroom door ajar, I could see the front counter. Mr. Buffington was on the phone. He hung up and brung me a clean dust rag and roll of tape. He told me to bandage the cut to stem the bleeding and keep my arm raised. By the time I had wrapped my hand, he had gathered the broken glass and was mopping. I noticed he had a hobble.

"Sit still until Martha gets here," he said, pointing to a chair near the end of the counter.

He spread the newspaper and stood and read for quite a stretch. He chuckled onc't, and when he folded the paper, I seen he was reading the funnies. A few customers come in who looked like they had already worked a full day even though it was only noon. One of them had dark stains on his shirt, and his fingernails was mostly black. His eyes fixed on me while he waited in line. I squirmed.

The next time the door opened, a lady walked in, and I supposed she was in the wrong place. The look on her face told me she had a similar thought about me. A boy in an army-green jacket held the door for her. His hair was short, and he wore a class ring, like the one Bobby Blaylock twisted backwards for thumping underclassmen on the head.

Mr. Buffington put the paper aside. "My Lord, they buzzed you good, son."

The boy had a big grin and run his hand across his hair, like he was still getting used to how it felt.

"You'll make one hell of a soldier."

The boy smiled big again.

The lady placed two brown bags in front of Mr. Buffington. He said something, and they both glanced at me. She walked toward me carrying one bag and set it on the floor, then knelt and held my hand. Her skin was soft. She removed the tape and slowly peeled back the cloth. It was a deep red.

"You poor thing." She took a fresh towel to the sink and wet the corner with warm water. She wiped away the dried blood and patted the cut with the dry part of the cloth. It hurt, but I didn't flinch.

"You ought to have stitches." She turned to Mr. Buffington. "He needs stitches."

"Just do the best you can, Martha."

The boy walked up and looked over her shoulder. "I'd be crying like a baby. You must be tough as nails." He leaned down and let me feel his hair. It was prickly.

Mrs. Buffington reached in the bag for a tube of gel. She squeezed the tube, running the tip along the end of her finger, then rubbed gel on my palm. She stuck three Band-Aides across the gash and explained how they would hold the skin together so it could heal. She had to remind me to pay attention because I kept staring at her. That was the first time I remembered being attracted to a woman.

When she had finished, she give me the gel and extra Band-Aides and told me to replace the bandages later that evening. She left with the boy, and Mr. Buffington pulled out two sandwiches from the other bag and tossed me one. After lunch, he had me straighten bottles, dust shelves, and break down boxes. Mrs. Buffington filled my mind the whole time.

Twenty minutes past close, we knowed Ricky weren't coming, so Mr. Buffington drove me home. He didn't say nothing until we stopped at the house. "I'll be here at eight, sharp."

I climbed from the truck and shut the door.

That night, I learnt Ricky had fed Mom bull about Mr. Buffington needing help at the store. I didn't tell her no different. And when I said Mr. Buffington wanted me all week, Ricky's lie growed teeth. Mom weren't too keen on the idea—especially when I explained how I had hurt myself taking out trash—but she finally agreed.

Mr. Buffington picked me up and dropped me off every day that week. I helped him stock and organize and clean. When he showed me how to run the cash register, I seen the sawed-off shotgun mounted beneath the counter, and he told me about the time he had blowed the glass out of his own door stopping a man who had robbed him. My eyes got big. "A little scratch ain't so bad, eh?" he said.

Several men had visited Mr. Buffington throughout the week, and they had spun yarns and laughed and called him Buckshot, but I didn't piece it together until hearing about the robber. I wondered if Ricky had knowed that story when he had hatched his plan.

On Saturday, when Mr. Buffington brung me home, I looked out the window during the ride. He remained quiet until we pulled in the drive.

"You worked hard this week. And nobody works for me for free." He slid me a five-dollar bill. I stretched it full-length between my thumbs. The fact I had never held five dollars of my own weren't lost on him. "Put that in your pocket."

"Yes sir." I folded it and done as he said.

"I could use your help next week too. I'll check with your mother."

I smiled and reached for the door.

"Donny," Mr. Buffington said, and something about his voice caught my attention. I held still, fingers wrapped around the handle. "You ain't got to steal for him."

I paused a moment longer, then opened the door and jumped out. Ricky was standing in the yard, and Mr. Buffington stuck his head from the driver-side window. "You ever set foot in my store, you son of a bitch, I'll shoot your sorry ass." He drove away. I smiled again.

Now, as I stared across that field, watching them grasshoppers and thinking about the look on Ricky's face when Mr. Buffington had threatened him, I heard Abigail say something.

"Do what?" I said.

"Should we clean up the broken glass?"

I recalled Mr. Buffington mopping that spilt whiskey again. Then I remembered how not long ago he was shot and killt when someone had robbed the liquor store.

"Ain't our problem." I walked to the truck and emptied the spent casings and reloaded the .38. I liked how snug them cartridges fit in each chamber. I flicked my wrist, clamping the cylinder shut, and laid the revolver in the glovebox.

I run my thumb over the palm of my hand and looked at the scar. No, I thought again, I sure as hell don't like Ricky at all.

Jesse III

A Crooked Heart

Pop was different after Mamma held that gun on him. He never brung up my missed tackles again, but he didn't mention nothing else about the football games neither. I wondered if he liked going to them at all. He worked at Fred's until late and went deer hunting every weekend. When he stayed home, he was either outside or watching TV. And if he ate with me and Mamma, usually the only sounds was silverware scraping plates and glasses tapping the table.

We had never talked about the night Mamma fired the shot, but even though Pop hadn't laid a hand on us since then, the tension was worse. I could tell Mamma felt it too.

"How was work today?" Mamma said one evening near Christmas.

"Fine."

"What'd you do?"

Pop's fork rattled when he dropped it, and his face was blank when he looked up. "Work."

Mamma pinched a smile. "I know you worked, but how was it?"

"Done told you. Fine." He scooted his chair from the table and walked to the living room. I heard the TV click on. I looked at Mamma, and now her face was blank. She stood and cleared his plate.

While she washed dishes, I spread newspaper on the table. I lifted the lid off a box and separated loose parts to the model car I had been building during Christmas break. I opened the instructions and studied the pictures. Then I glued the exhaust manifold to the engine block.

The phone rung.

On the third ring, Mamma glanced over her shoulder. I raised the glued pieces, holding them steady.

"Donny, can you get that?" The phone rung again. "Donny!"

He grumbled as he moseyed to the kitchen. By the way he answered, I was surprised the caller didn't hang up. Pop turned his back to me. "How the hell are you?" He stepped into the next room, stretching the pigtail.

Water stopped sloshing as Mamma froze, her hands still in the sink. Pop never got phone calls, and we both listened. When he spoke, he didn't sound gruff no more— and then he laughed loud. Me and Mamma looked at each other. She wrinkled her brow.

When Pop hung up, Mamma asked who it was.

"None of your goddamn business."

Mamma faced him, pointing her finger, water dripping from her hand. "Don't you dare take the Lord's name in vain under my roof!"

Pop's eyes narrowed. "Whose roof?"

Mamma lowered her hand, and they glared, motionless. I held my breath, ready to drop them model pieces.

Pop grinned. "I'm just joshin', Abigail." He walked from the kitchen and come back holding his hunting rifle. He propped it by the door. "I'll be gone tomorrow."

"Tomorrow? What about work?"

"Murry and Fred can handle it."

"That's not the point. We're scraping by as it is."

Pop sniffed. "Ain't much to do right now nohow." He strode out, and I heard him rummaging through the closet.

Water splashed as Mamma scrubbed a plate. She dried the dishes and went to the living room and switched channels. The weatherman mentioned a cold front as the last of the dishwater gurgled down the drain.

Maybe it was because I was building a model hotrod, or maybe their argument triggered it, but I remembered the first time I had felt tension between them. I was twelve. They had fought in the car on the way home, and Mamma had dropped off Pop and drove us to Tammy Weldon's house. Mamma had talked to Tammy at the door, then led me inside to the couch. Dark brown paneling walled the room, and the house smelled like pennies.

Tammy's son piled Matchbox cars on the floor and then slouched in an armchair. I slid from the couch and sorted through them. David was older than me, and I figured he stayed in the room to make sure I didn't hurt nothing.

I tried not to think about the fight between Mamma and Pop. I had the feeling David could see through me somehow, and I didn't want him reading my thoughts. So I lined the cars beside each other and pretended to have fun.

A little girl plopped in front of me and rolled a car back and forth in a half-circle. Then she shoved it. The car streaked across the short carpet and slammed into a baseboard.

"Careful," David said.

She reached for another one and looked at me. "I'm Katheryn."

"I know."

Her eyes growed big. "How did you know?"

"You told me. At church."

"Oh. What's your name?"

"Jesse."

"Oh. What's your real name?"

I wasn't sure what to say, so I told her my name again.

"She means your last name."

I glanced at her brother and turned back toward Katheryn. She was staring at me.

"Hartline."

"Oh. Hartline like a heart?" She pointed to her chest. "I can make a heart." She skipped from the room and hurried back with paper and a fistful of crayons. She set a piece of paper on the carpet. The corners lifted as she drawed.

She held up a crooked heart. I said it was perfect, and she stuck out her tongue.

"Katheryn," David said.

She laid the paper on the floor and colored her drawing, getting outside the lines, then gave me a crayon, so I helped. Our crayons tapped, and she giggled. She started hitting mine on purpose. She laughed every time. When she pressed too hard, a hole tore in the paper, so she crawled to a small table with a lamp on it and stood on her knees to color. I pitched my crayon with the others, and she glanced sideways at me, raising her hand to the lampshade. Her brother said her name again, and she lowered the crayon.

"Want to see something cool?" David went down the hall and returned holding a model car. I jumped up, and he handed it to me. It was a hotrod with part of the engine coming through the hood. The car was black and had flames stretching from the fenders to the doors. The wheels and bumpers was shiny.

Katheryn come up for a closer look, and David's arm shot out to hold her back. She stood on her tiptoes and placed her hands on his forearm, like she was peeking over the top rail of a fence.

"You can have it," he said.

I imagined it on my shelf. "Really?"

He nodded.

"Can I have it too?" Katheryn said.

Her brother smiled. "How about we just let Jesse have it?"

"Jesse Hartline like a heart?"

He nodded again.

I gently set the model next to the lamp. Katheryn fetched a doll and put its feet on two cars and pretended they was roller skates. I crossed my legs beside her and played. I kept glancing at the hotrod.

After a while, Mamma come in the room and told me it was time to go. I showed her the model. "Look what David gave me!"

She eyed the car. "You shouldn't take his toys."

"It's not a toy. It's a model."

"No sir," Mamma said. "Please give it back." She touched David's arm. "That's sweet of you, David, but you should keep it."

The hotrod felt heavy as I handed it to him.

Katheryn hopped up and stepped between me and David, her face raised toward her brother. "Now can I have it?"

"No," David said. "It's for boys."

"Oh." Her bottom lip pouted, and her shoulders dropped. Then she looked up with wide eyes and leaned forward. "Maybe I can have it sometimes?"

David put a hand on her head, his fingers splayed. "Maybe sometimes."

She patted his hand with both of hers, then went to the table and colored.

We was saying goodbye at the door when Katheryn slipped me a piece of paper and scampered away, her bare feet smacking the floor. I unfolded it. She had drawed another heart. It wasn't as crooked as the first one, but she had colored outside the lines again.

For the next two years, whenever I seen Katheryn at church she would say, "Hey Jesse Hartline like a heart", and now and then she would bring me a folded piece of paper. Each heart was a different color.

One Sunday while everybody was talking in the churchyard, Katheryn hid behind Tammy when I tried to catch her attention. I changed my angle, and she slid further around her mother's legs. Tammy smiled and, leaning down, said something to her.

Then everything went black as my face was buried in a mushy bosom. Crushed by a bearhug, I knew Brenda Allen had snuck up on me. Brenda was one of Mamma's friends, but I always dodged her. She had wrapped her flabby arms around me so fast I didn't have time to take my hands out of my pockets. She squeezed me to the point where I could hardly breathe.

"I've been praying for you," she said, and I could tell she had started crying by how she shook. I was glad I couldn't see nothing because I felt like everyone was watching. When she finally let go, she grabbed a tissue from her purse and wiped tears from her eyes. I lowered my head and hurried to the car.

On the drive home, I told Mamma I hated the way Brenda hugged me. She said I should be thankful people cared about us. But to me, it seemed like Brenda only cared when she could put on a show.

I stared out the window and wondered what Mamma had told her friends and if they done stuff for us because they was sorry for how Pop treated us. Then I thought about Katheryn and all the folded papers she had brung me, and I realized her gifts come from someplace different.

Katheryn never gave me no more drawings once she turned shy. But sometimes when I felt low, I pulled out the colored hearts I had saved and spread them on the floor, and they always made me smile.

Now, as I held the plastic steering column to the dashboard, waiting for the glue to dry, I looked at the picture of the car on the box and recalled how me and Katheryn had both wanted David's model. I wondered if he had tried to give it to me because he had felt bad for me, and then I wondered if the hotrod had really been as perfect as I remembered.

A few days later, several inches of snow fell on Christmas Eve. Pop was at the shop, catching up from the days he had missed while hunting. Mamma said it was too cold to go outside, but she moved a chair beside a window and sat with her hands wrapped around a mug, watching the big flakes drift to the ground. She blowed the steaming coffee.

I bundled in layers of clothing. When Jake seen me holding my walking stick and wearing camouflage, he had a high-pitched bark. He spun circles and lunged at me, his tail wagging. Then he trotted across the yard, almost prancing, and when he turned toward me, it looked like he was smiling.

We went down the old logging road. Jake bolted ahead and run back a couple of times before it struck me he didn't make noise. Usually dead leaves crunched and rustled as I walked and Jake followed scents.

Rabbit tracks crossed the road, leading to a brush pile, and Jake dove in nose first. He sniffed and whined. When he pulled his head out, I seen his breath as he panted, and chunks of snow clung to his fur. He shook from head to tail.

I stopped where the road ended. Normally, the ridgelines blended together in leaf brown, but the snow brung out the lay of the land, and I could see the three spurs leading to the top of the hill. The trail to my campsite was covered, but I hiked the hidden path to the saddle of two ridges.

A ring of rocks made a round hump on the ground, and I stooped to clear the center of the firepit. I gathered twigs from trees and built a type of teepee and then added bigger sticks, leaving a hollow on the bottom, so I could reach inside. I slid a box from my pocket, struck a match, and held it to the kindling. On the second try, the flame took, and it climbed and spread as the wood crackled. I snapped dead limbs from trees and stacked them beside the rocks.

Two stumps stood near the fire. Me and Evan had carried them to the campsite after we had growed tired of sitting on the ground. I brushed one off and sat, then held out my hands and felt the warmth through my cloth gloves. The falling flakes disappeared as they landed in the fire, and before long, the damp wood hissed, and the snow on the heated stones started melting.

As I stared at the flames, random thoughts crossed my mind: how a football was harder to grip in the cold, decorating the Christmas tree with Mamma, how winter settled the dust. Then I thought about school. After this semester, I would have to earn a living. I could keep pumping gas and fixing cars, but I didn't want to spend my days with Pop at the garage. The work was harder, but I would rather be at the sawmill. Or maybe I would do both jobs again and save enough money to go where nobody knew nothing about me and I wouldn't be uneasy in my own home. One place come to mind, and I wondered what Number 9 bridge looked like in the snow, how fast the train had been going when Evan had jumped on board, and if I would have the nerve to follow him to Birmingham.

Jake rested his muzzle on my thigh. I scratched behind his ears. Then I stoked the fire with the last of the wood. It blazed and popped, shooting embers in different directions as sparks rose. I watched the flames until they died down, then scooped handfuls of snow on the hot coals. The firepit sizzled and smoked.

Back in the yard, I went to Jake's water bucket and broke the ice with my walking stick and removed the frozen layer. I shivered when my hand touched the water. My glove was soaked, and my clothes smelled of woodsmoke.

I was watching Jake drink when a snowball nailed my cheekbone and busted apart. I jerked my head around, expecting to see Pop. Mamma was doubled over. When I seen she had throwed it, I wasn't mad no more. I pulled my toboggin off and slapped it against my leg.

"I didn't mean to hit you," she said, still laughing. She covered her mouth with her hand, but she couldn't hide her smile.

When I bent down, Mamma yelped and hustled for the house. I lobbed the snowball, and it landed on the doormat as she stepped inside. She peeked out just as I tossed another one, then ducked behind the door. It hit the frame and splattered. The door stayed shut. I picked up my stick and turned toward the house. Smoke trailed from the chimney, floating over the yard, and icicles lined the edge of the roof, dripping.

The snow had slacked by the time Pop come home. Me and Mamma was sitting at the table, sipping hot chocolate. I had hung my stocking and was working on the model while she wrapped presents.

Cold air blowed in the house when Pop stomped his boots at the door. "I checked on Granny."

"You should've brought her," Mamma said.

"She wanted to stay home." He rubbed his palm. "The roads is bad, but I promised we'd come over tomorrow."

Mamma said it was supposed to warm up but we could hoof it if we had to. "Like an old-fashioned Christmas," she said.

"What about your folks?"

"I told Mother we would play it by ear."

"Will Aunt Jackie be there?" I said.

"Not this year. Maybe next." Aunt Jackie hadn't visited for Christmas in several years, and I could tell Mamma wasn't convinced about next year neither. She handed Pop a present. "Put this under the tree."

He read the nametag and shook his gift. Something thudded. "A rock," he said, and strode out.

Mamma placed another box on the table and cut the wrapping paper with scissors. Tape screeched as she pulled a strip, then she folded the paper around the box. She sighed. "I always wanted a white Christmas, but I never considered it would mean not being with family."

Pop poked his head in the kitchen. "You are with family."

Later, beneath thick blankets, I laid in bed thinking about my favorite Christmas gifts over the years—a trainset, army men, a BB gun—and how I used to have a hard time falling asleep the night before Christmas. My thoughts drifted to the campsite and the ring of steaming rocks, the shifting colors of the glowing embers, the stump capped in snow. Aunt Jackie and Uncle Dewayne come to mind. Then I remembered what Pop had said about family, how Mamma had looked at him and smiled, and how different that smile had been from when she had hit me with the snowball.

Abigail III

White Trash

I turned toward Jackie and her boyfriend, who sat holding hands in the back seat. Donny and I had taken them to the car show for my sister's birthday, and we had stopped for ice cream on the way home. Jackie had finished her cone, but Dewayne was still drinking his milkshake.

"Did you have fun?"

Jackie nodded, and Dewayne said, "Yes ma'am".

I smiled. "You don't have to call me ma'am. I'm only a few years older than you."

"Five for me—as of today," Jackie said.

"Boy's got respect," Donny said. "Don't learn him no different."

"I liked the old-timey cars best," Jackie said. "Because of the horn."

"Them Mustangs was tough." Dewayne slurped the last of his milkshake through his straw.

"Boy's got good taste in cars too." Donny glanced in the rearview mirror. "Know what makes a car fast?"

"The horsepower," Dewayne said.

Donny gunned the engine and sped up, then slowed. "The driver." Dewayne grinned.

"Do it again!" Jackie said.

"Are you finished?" I said, pointing at Dewayne's cup.

"Yes ma'am."

I placed his cup in the bag, folded the top closed, and set it in the middle of the seat. Donny reached for it, then rolled down his window.

"Don't throw that out!"

His face reddened, and he looked sideways at me. He grabbed the bottom of the bag and held it out the window. I figured he was just trying to fluster me, but then he turned it over and shook it, spilling both cups, my bowl and plastic spoon, and all the napkins. The bag rattled in the wind. I watched the litter scatter on the road behind us. Dewayne smiled, but Jackie's mouth had dropped open. The breeze blew her hair across her face.

Donny handed me the empty bag. "There," he said, "I didn't throw it out."

"I can't believe you did that!"

Donny sniffed. "Take heed, young buck. Give a woman what she wants, and she still finds a reason to complain."

Dewayne's laugh was cut short when I shot an angry look at Donny. "We are *not* white trash."

He checked the mirror again. "You think I'm white trash?"

Dewayne was wide-eyed. He stammered.

"He's teasing you," I said, forcing a smile.

We took Jackie and Dewayne to my parents' house.

"You scared that poor boy half to death," I said, after we had waved goodbye.

Donny had a smirk and drove without a word. A mile or so from home, he pulled over and left the engine running. That was the first time we had been to town since our wedding, and I thought he wanted to kiss and make up, like when we had dated.

He faced me, propping his elbow on top of the seat. He held up his finger. "That's your one free pass. Don't never disrespect me in front of nobody. You hear?"

"You shouldn't litter," I said, then bit my lip.

He turned red again. "I'll throw out trash anytime I damn well please." He stretched across me and opened my door. I didn't budge. "Don't make this hard on yourself. Not in your condition."

I gritted my teeth and squeezed my thighs. Donny opened his door and walked to my side. I pictured him twisting my arm or dragging me by the hair, so I swung my feet around and placed them on the dirt. I noticed a broken bottle in the ditch.

"This'll give you time to contemplate what you done." He closed my door, strolled to the driver side, and then eased down the road, like he had dropped me off after a date.

I felt a knot in my throat. My legs almost folded beneath me, so I sat in the road and buried my face in my hands. My shoulders shook.

I wasn't sure how much time had passed when I heard a car. I wiped away my tears, stood, and swatted my dress. The dust still hovered as the car rounded the curve.

Gladdis Sumner slowed to a stop, and her passenger window lowered.

She leaned over. "Everything okay?"

I knew if I said something right then I would cry again, so I just nodded. She offered a ride, and I hesitated, not knowing what Donny would think, then I got in her car. I sunk in the comfortable seat. Mrs. Sumner pushed a button and raised my window. I tilted my head back and closed my eyes. The air conditioning cooled me.

She turned the gospel music down. "You shouldn't be walking in this heat."

I wondered if she had seen the bump of my stomach or had heard I was pregnant. "I ran out of gas," I said, glancing at her. I twiddled the fabric of my dress, then slid my hands across my lap to smooth the wrinkles. I took a deep breath. "Donny kicked me out of the car."

Mrs. Sumner stared ahead. Her expression didn't change. "I see," she said, nodding slowly. "A man who does that to his wife ought to be—"

I straightened up.

"I have no right," she said. "Family is family, and the greatest fault of us women is we put family first."

I looked at Mrs. Sumner, and this time, I actually noticed her features. She had wrinkles around her eyes, but she didn't look old. Her hair was perfect, like she had used a whole can of hairspray on it, and her heavy earrings pulled at her lobes. I had always assumed Mrs. Sumner had an easy life, but when I saw how the corner of her mouth frowned, it dawned on me she probably had her share of struggles too.

"Oh, sure," she said, "we say we put God first, but that's no longer true after getting married and carrying a baby. Children change your perspective."

I had never considered that before, but it struck me how I had already started thinking about my baby more than anything.

We passed a truck going the opposite direction and drove through its dust.

"Being a mother is both challenging and rewarding, and I have learned the hardest part is letting go."

Her daughter had left for school two months earlier. I was glad she was gone, but I decided to be polite. "Does Amy like college?"

Mrs. Sumner swerved to miss a pothole. "Donny is handsome," she said, "but I'll never understand why the smartest girl in class wasted so much time on that boy."

She didn't seem to realize she had insulted me. I couldn't say what Mrs. Sumner knew about Amy and Donny, but it sounded as though she thought Amy had dodged a bullet.

At the last straightaway before the house, I said, "I'll get out here".

Mrs. Sumner stopped the car, then reached for my hand and squeezed. "If you ever need anything," she said, "just ask." She looked me in the eye. "You're a mother now. Don't let pride interfere with your child's welfare."

I thanked her for the ride. As she pulled away, I watched the dust rise and drift through the trees at the edge of the woods. The leaves had started falling, but it was hot for October.

When I walked up the drive, Donny was swinging on the front porch, drinking a beer. He stood and hugged me. My stomach pressed against him, and I wrapped my arms around his waist. Sweat had soaked into the back of his shirt.

"Scripture says the husband rules the wife."

I nodded into his neck, remembering the rest of that passage, which I knew he couldn't quote.

I sat on the swing and looked toward the road. Donny went inside, and the screen door smacked the frame behind him. When he returned, he handed me iced tea. Beads of sweat had formed on the glass. I sipped it and traced the cold to my stomach. Donny draped his arm over my shoulder, and I leaned into him. The chains creaked as we swung. A few leaves had blown onto the porch. They still held their autumn colors.

I thought about my conversation with Mrs. Sumner, and I determined, from then on, whatever happened between Donny and me would stay between Donny and me. Then I recalled her comment, and I knew two things for certain: I would always need plenty, and I would never ask her for anything.

Donny III

Red Dresses

Over the years, the Sumner barn had started leaning toward the creek at the foot of the field. Jim had told me he didn't trust it no more but still needed it to store hay for his fifty head of cattle. He paid by the hour—and paid good to boot—so I took my time and done the job right. The summer after Jesse graduated had been dry in July and hotter in August, so I had swung a deal with Fred where I went to Jim's in the mornings when it was cooler and made up the hours at the shop in the evenings. Fred knowed I was hurting for money, so he hadn't fought me none. Plus, the long days kept me out of the house and away from Abigail's nagging.

I had worked on the barn for a week—using jacks, Jim's tractor, and pullies to straighten it—and I had set up braces while replacing the support beams. Then I had hammered extra nails in the joists and repaired the steps to the landing.

I was now walking the loft, inspecting the floor. Several bales of hay was scattered, so I toted them to the edge and flung them down. The twine snapped from a couple of bales when they landed, spilling hay.

While I judged how much lumber I'd need, two young boys come in right below me. I watched them through the gaps in the flooring until they stepped into the open. I heard them planning to make the barn their secret hideout.

The wind had blowed all morning, so I had growed used to the tin roof making a racket. But when a gust peeled back the loose corner of metal and it slammed down, both them boys jumped. I didn't want nobody nosing around and getting in my way, so I hollered at them. The little one grabbed the other boy's arm. When they seen me standing over them, the taller boy said Mr. Sumner was their granddad. I told them to get the hell out. They left so fast dust hung in the air where they had stood.

I couldn't help but laugh. I figured I had done the same thing years ago when Jim had almost found me with his daughter. Shortly after me and Amy had climbed in the loft one night, the old bay had nickered, giving me just enough warning to slip on my boots and escape out the back as Jim had busted in the front. While I sprinted across the field, he had yelled Amy's boyfriend's name, which had made me smile. But I was all business when the shotgun had gone off. Splashing through the creek toward the truck with my clothes bundled in the crook of my arm, I had felt like a football player again—running for my life, adrenaline pumping. The only time I had that feeling nowadays was when I fought or gambled, but I hadn't been in a scrap for a while.

Since Amy had been dating Greg while I was with Abigail, the Sumner barn had been the best place for us to meet. She'd be reclined on a blanket when I crept in. We'd see each other a couple nights a week, and although we had a few close shaves with her father, Jim never caught us. But then Amy had cut me off after I had thumped Greg. I would've done whatever it took to get her back, but Abigail had ruint everything by getting pregnant.

I knowed Jim had heard about that mess with me and Amy and Greg, but he hadn't let on at the time, and he had never mentioned it since.

The wind lifted the corner of the roof again, and the metal banged against the rafters. I went to where it flapped. The tin had rusted through and tore from the nails, and the wood was rot.

When I walked in the barn the next day, a girl with long blonde hair was laying on the hay that had spilt. She had spread out a blanket. For an instant, I thought it was Amy, and it seemed like I had stepped twenty years in the past. I stopped dead in my tracks.

The girl was reading a book and cut her eyes toward me. "You frightened my brothers."

It took a second to get my mind to the present, and I realized she was talking about them two boys from the day before.

"They think you're the devil," she said, "so this is the only place I can come without them pestering me."

I strode by the girl and draped my tool belt over the end of the sawhorse. "Are you scared too?" I heard the difference in my voice from when I had run off her brothers.

She was still reading, but she finally lowered her book and met my eyes when she spoke. "I'm not afraid of the devil."

That hellcat Amy flashed through my mind again, and I looked hard at the girl. "You take after your mother."

She smiled and went back to reading.

We didn't say nothing else, but I caught her cutting her eyes at me now and again, and one time she was staring over her book and playing with her necklace. I stayed until she left.

The next morning, I woke early and drove to the Sumner's. I worked hard the first few hours, but I kept glancing toward the door. When my coffee was gone, I broke off a plug of tobacco, then climbed the steps to the loft and tugged on a warped piece of flooring with my crowbar. Them nails clung tight and squeaked loud as I pumped the wood back and forth, and they was bent and warm after I pulled the plank free. I dropped the board from the landing, and dust flew when it hit the ground. Them crooked nails was sticking up.

The door creaked open beneath me.

"I was wonderin' if you'd come today."

"Wanted to see what I'm paying you for." Jim's voice sent a jolt through me. I hadn't seen him since he had hired me. If he noticed anything different in how I sounded, I bet he thought I was just nervous about not having the barn finished.

I hustled down the steps and showed him the work I had done. He studied the ridge board and followed it to the gables. "Straight and sturdy," he said, patting a support beam.

We went outside, and I pointed to the part of the roof needing replaced. He handed me money for supplies. As we talked beside his truck, a curtain was pulled aside in one of the upper windows of the house. Then it closed.

"Good job, Donny. Once the roof is repaired, she'll be in fine shape."

"Yes sir. She'll be ready to hold whatever you put in her."

We shook hands, and he drove across the field and up his driveway, a cloud of dust behind him. I glanced at the house and seen that curtain open again. I spat tobacco juice and stepped in the barn.

I was nailing a piece of flooring when I heard the hinges. This time I peeked through the gap in the planks.

The girl come in and latched the door. She had on another dress, and her hair was hanging over one shoulder. I had piled more hay for her. She laid the blanket on it and stuck her nose in the book. We picked up where we had left off: She cut her eyes at me throughout the morning, and it took me twiced as long to get stuff done.

A few hours later, the last two boards for the loft was laying on the sawhorses. I measured one and marked it, then spat.

"That's gross."

I grinned. I tucked the carpenter pencil behind my ear and walked toward her. "You was a lot cuter when you kept your mouth shut." I crossed the dirt floor and opened the door. Hooking my finger in my cheek, I raked out the tobacco and slung it in the field. On the way back, I stopped in front of her. "Happy?"

She nodded onc't.

I gripped the saw handle, but the other end of the board hopped when I tried to get a bite in the wood. I pushed it further back on the sawhorse and dug the saw's teeth in the mark. This time it felt too stable. I paused and looked down the length of the board. The girl was leaning over the backend with her fingers wrapped around the sides, using her weight to hold it steady. Her necklace hung low, and the top of her dress puckered. She locked her eyes on mine.

"That's a purty necklace."

She leaned down further.

All the time she had been reading, I had thought she was trying to get my attention. She'd play with her hair, bend her knee so her dress would inch up her leg, and lick her finger to turn pages. But now I was certain she knowed what she was doing. My stomach fluttered—that same rush I used to get before football games. Coach had called it butterflies, which sounded like sissy talk, but I didn't know no better way to put it.

I stared down her dress. She never flinched.

I shifted my focus to the wood and sawed back and forth until the block fell to the dirt. I thumbed the edge. The cut was clean.

The girl settled on the blanket and read. When she knowed I was watching, she wet her finger and turned a page. "Don't you ever take a break?"

I lifted the plank and propped it against the landing, then shoved it into the loft. "Don't need no break."

"Too bad."

I measured the other board, drawed a dark line, and laid down my pencil. "Why come?"

She stood and dropped her book on the blanket. "Because I want a break." She didn't pay me no mind until she stopped and swung the door open. "You're boring," she said over her shoulder, and stepped out. The sunrays slanting through the doorway caught flecks of dust.

Now that girl had come in and out of the barn several times over the last two days, and she had never left the door open. I felt them butterflies. I run my hand across my whiskers and went outside. When my eyes adjusted to the light, I seen her crossing the field. I rubbed my chin again. I didn't see nobody at the house. I looked at the girl and back toward the house, then followed her to the creek.

I sat beside a boulder shaped like a wedge. It angled down from the bank with only its tip in the stream, but I knowed during floods the water rose and wrapped around the whole thing.

She slid from them sandals and stepped barefoot in the creek, holding her dress above her knees. Water eddied around her tan legs as bright flashes reflected off ripples in the stream. The girl's hair glowed.

She cut her eyes at me and smiled, then took a couple more steps and—even though it weren't no deeper—slowly pulled her dress higher. It hung in folds in the front and back, but she gathered the sides of it in her fingers, sliding her hands up her thighs. She held still, and only her lips moved. I felt myself leaning toward her, but her voice blended with the sound of water. Then, just when I thought she was done, her hands eased above her thighs, and I seen where her bathing suit had left a tan line at her hip.

Chill bumps covered her long legs, and when she turned toward me, I noticed two larger bumps through the front of her dress. She kept her head down but raised her eyes and met mine. This time when she smiled, I seen the look in her eyes, and I knowed the true devil wore red dresses.

Book II

Jesse IV

Unsplit Wood

When Billy Tucker was shot at the sawmill, I thought that would be the end of it. I figured Earle would go to jail or Billy would kill him first chance he got. The bad blood between them had come to a boil this morning, and Earle had stormed off after they had argued. When he returned a few hours later—according to coworkers—he had the gun cinched in his belt and stunk of whiskey.

I didn't see it, but I heard the shot. I assumed Earle's truck had backfired since a moment later he sped away, so I had kept milling timber. But after four or five men run toward the lumberyard, I had shut off the saw and followed.

A crowd had gathered around Billy. He was laying on the ground cradling his arm, blood seeping into his shirt. When he sat up, his mouth twitched, and he mumbled something about being square. He started wheezing. Jeremiah cut off Billy's sleeve with his pocketknife and tied it around the wound. It looked like the bullet had just nicked him, but I seen pain on Billy's face when two men heaved him to his feet.

Jeremiah supported Billy as they shuffled to the office, and everybody stood beside the stained dirt, shaking heads and telling rumors. The story involving a woman made the most sense, but the one about Billy plowing over Earle's dog had some grip too.

I went and fired up the ripsaw. Sweat drenched my shirt. I pulled the rag hanging from my pocket and snapped it and wiped my face, then stepped from beneath the shed, staring at the sky. He'll forget, I thought.

The blade whirred behind me as my mind wandered. After graduation, I had started working for Billy again while pumping gas on weekends. I had also helped Mr. Smith truck several loads of hay. I wanted to save enough money to leave home by the end of August. The summer had been rainy at first, then turned hot and dry in July, and August had brung a heatwave. But the sky was overcast today. As I watched the clouds shift, I decided even if Billy forgot to tell me one way or the other, I'd knock off early.

Two days ago, Mr. Sumner had stopped at the filling station, and I had recognized them boys as soon as they had jumped out of his car. I had hustled to the pumps. The front seat was empty. Mr. Sumner had told me to fill it up, then propped against the car roof, staring toward the field as I pumped his gas. I wondered if he worried the grass was too dry to make good hay.

"Need rain."

He nodded.

I shaded my eyes. "Them boys have growed." He seemed deep in thought. I glanced at the numbers on the dial. "How long they in town?"

He took off his hat, reshaping the brim, then put it back on. About the time I figured he either hadn't heard or ignored me, he said, "Through Tuesday".

I didn't know what else to say unless I flat out asked if she had come too. I faced the field but kept my eye on him.

He checked his watch. The band glinted. "I understand you finished school."

We was headed down the wrong road. "Yes sir." The handle clicked off, and I hung the nozzle on the pump. I kneeled and tightened the gas cap.

"My grandbaby graduated too."

I sprung up as quick as that panel had clapped shut. The question was on the tip of my tongue when he said, "Where're you goin' to college?".

I shook my head. I had always supposed college was for folks who made better grades and had more money.

"Military?"

"No sir."

He frowned, and I hoped I hadn't hindered my chances of courting his granddaughter. I thought about telling him I was moving to Birmingham soon, or fib and say I was considering a junior college, but he looked past me and hollered, "Did you buy a Co' Cola for Sister?".

I felt a rush. I turned as the smaller boy held up an unopened bottle. He clutched a half-empty bottle in his other hand. My heart beat faster, and I thought: Only three days.

The brothers fought over the front seat as Mr. Sumner paid me, and the one holding his sister's Coke finally climbed in the back.

Mr. Sumner cranked the car and rested his elbow on the open window. "Plan your future, son, or you'll end up like"—he adjusted his hat—"other folks 'round here."

I read between the lines, but with Savannah in town, my future didn't go beyond Tuesday. I remembered how she had stood with one leg bent, hand cupped above her eyes, glowing in the sun.

The service bell rung, and the boy in the back seat looked at me through the rear window, his sweaty bangs matted to his brow. When the car was out of sight, I realized I had forgot to scrub the windshield.

So this morning, as soon as I had seen Billy at the sawmill, I had put in for half a day. He had asked me to check with him later, but now he was probably more concerned about patching up his arm. I would kick myself if I didn't do nothing, so at noon I went to the office, told Linda I had the afternoon off, and clocked out. My timing would be perfect if I got to the Sumner's after lunch since Pop would be at Fred's by then. I hopped on my bike and rode home. In the shower, I washed my hair twice and run my fingernail in the hollow of my ears, removing all the sawdust. I dressed in a clean shirt and jeans.

Distant thunder rumbled when I left the house, and a breeze cooled the air. I looked at the grey clouds. The one day I don't want rain, I thought. I pedaled slow along the winding roads, so I wouldn't get as sweaty, and pushed my bike up the steep hill where the old cabin had burned. Small trees had growed around the stone chimney. I passed the cemetery. At the last curve before the Sumner's, the woods met a clearing where the fence started. I heard a familiar truck and waited, using my foot for a kickstand. A dried mudpuddle was in the road, and deep cracks zigzagged the red dirt, breaking it apart in sections of smooth, hard clay.

A peal of thunder rolled overhead as the mailman slowed to a stop beside me. Dust from his truck blowed through the trees. His Red Man cap was pushed back on his head, the bill dirty. He flicked his finger toward the sky. "Need a lift?"

As he stared, I thought it might be weird to show up unannounced at the Sumner's. I wasn't sure what to say when someone opened the door, but I knew I wouldn't ask Savannah on a date if Mrs. Sumner and them boys was gawking at me. Then it struck me Mr. Sumner might be home too, and his frown come to mind.

Mr. Blevins raised his eyebrows.

I was fixing to load my bike in his truck when suddenly I recalled what Evan had said about me growing a pair. I gripped the handlebars. "I'm good."

Mr. Blevins scratched above his ear, and his hat shifted. "Suit yourself." The transmission clunked when he jammed it in gear, and I knew he needed to check the mount or the fluid. He leaned and spat. "Tell your daddy to watch his step."

I noticed tobacco stains on the door as I wondered what Pop had done to get on his bad side.

The bald tires found traction somehow, and he rattled up the road. Probably the fluid, I thought.

I smelled rain.

I decided to tell Mrs. Sumner I got caught in the storm and needed to call Mamma for a ride, so I laid my bike at the edge of the woods. A layer of dust covered the leaves.

I walked along the road and out of the curve. The white Sumner house seemed to glow beneath the dark clouds. I could only see the top of the barn since the land sloped from the house to the creek. I had rinsed in the creek once after unloading a truckload of hay, right before Mrs. Sumner brung lemonade.

Lightning flashed, and thunder boomed so close it vibrated me. I run toward the house. Halfway there, the property come into full view, and I glanced across the fields— then skidded to a stop.

Pop's truck was parked at the barn. A ladder leaned against the eaves, a square hole in the bottom corner of the roof. The new sheets Pop had hung was shiny compared to the burned orange of the old tin, and the hole looked black. The near pasture was empty, but a dark red bull stood on the other side of the fence, staring at the barn. Its shoulder muscles bulged in ripples. A wad of cows huddled under trees in the lower field. Toward the creek, a streaked wall of grey moved steady across the pasture, growing louder. The smooth surface of the pond started churning, and everything faded in the downpour.

A bolt of lightning struck nearby, and I seen a wisp of black smoke where it had been. Sprinkles pattered leaves, and big drops kicked up poofs of dust in the road. I sprinted, then the wall of rain caught me. By the time I made it to the driveway, the potholes had turned to puddles. I splashed through them and jumped on the porch. My shirt was plastered to my skin, and I got goose bumps. Red mud covered my shoes.

I slung my head and rubbed my face. I felt the mixture of sweat, oil, and water.

Pop had ruined my plan, and now I would have to say he told me to call Mamma to pick me up, which didn't sound convincing—especially with him fixing to head out.

I dripped on the welcome mat and imagined Savannah inviting me inside and giving me a towel. I still didn't know the best way to ask her on a date, but I cleared my throat, held my fist steady, and tapped the door. I run my fingers through my hair and hoped she wouldn't recognize me from the filling station. As I waited, I noticed mud I had tracked on the porch, and I swiped a clod off with the side of my foot. It smeared. Rain hammered the roof and blowed on me. The wicker rocking chair turned a deeper brown.

I knocked harder, then wiped my clammy hand on my jeans. I had paced several lengths of the porch when it struck me no cars was in the drive. I peeked in the window beside the door. The room was dark, but I seen armchairs, a fireplace, and bookshelves.

I heard my breath as I let it out. I walked to the end of the porch, hands on my hips. The patch of grass between the house and pasture was dying, and, near the gate, coiled barbed wire hung from a fencepost. It was rusted. The barn looked blurry, and the water draining from the tin roof was broken apart by the ladder. I thought about how Pop only took care of his own tools. The bull hadn't budged. Neither had the truck, and I figured Pop was twiddling his thumbs, waiting for the rain to slack.

At this point, the only way I would see Savannah was with Pop. Yesterday, he had told me to prepare a cord of firewood for Mr. Sumner, so now I decided to take tomorrow morning off from the sawmill and deliver the first load with him. If I acted nervous around Savannah, Pop would probably tease me about being in love, but I could handle his razzing if I scored a date. I hoped she would bring me a glass of homemade lemonade after I stacked the wood. I peered in the window once more and pictured her standing there, her blonde hair in a braid, fingering her necklace, eyeing me as she drunk that Coke.

The lightning had passed, but the rain had settled in. I stepped off the porch, glanced toward the barn, and trudged to the woods. The dust had washed from the leaves, and they was green again. I lugged my bike to the road, splashing through the orange stream in the ditch. Mud splattered all over my back as I pedaled home.

*

The next morning, I woke before sunrise. The old oak near my window turned from black to grey as the day brightened.

When I rolled out of bed, Pop was already outside, and Mamma was cooking breakfast. She asked me to fetch the eggs. I slipped my shoes on, and when I stepped in the chicken coop, the hens went to squawking. I swatted Thelma from her nest, and she flapped her wings to the ground. Tufts of feathers she had shed floated in the air. By the time I returned with the basket, the smell of bacon filled the house as it sizzled and popped in the skillet.

I thumbed through the phonebook while Mamma cracked eggs on the lip of a bowl and piled the speckled shells on the counter. I could tell she wondered who I was calling as I dialed the sawmill's number.

Linda answered but made a comment to somebody in the background before saying hello. I told her I would be late because I had to help Pop with a few chores. "Just lay it on the chair," Linda said. "What's that, Jesse?" I repeated it, Mamma giving me a look over her shoulder as she stirred the eggs. When I hung up, I asked if she had heard about Billy, which was the best distraction I could think of, and we discussed it during breakfast. She said the diner would be buzzing with gossip.

As I ate bacon, I realized Mamma was watching.

"You should've called me after work yesterday."

I stopped midchew.

"Your shirt was a sight."

I swallered, glad she hadn't noticed I had changed clothes. "The rain cured them wrinkles you was so worried about."

Her eyes didn't crinkle, so her smile looked sad. She sipped coffee and set the mug on the table. "Have you given thought to what you told me?"

I had, but I shook my head.

The screen door smacked, and bootheels tapped the wood floor. Pop had stood on the porch to eat. He hardly sat no more. His dishes clattered when he dropped them in the sink. Mamma cringed.

I dodged him whenever possible, so I shooed a fly from my plate and ate my toast as I walked outside. I moved the truck to the woodpile and started loading. The first few logs banged against the empty bed. I didn't stack none next to the cab since the metal was rusted out.

Mamma waved as she drove off for work. I watched the car go down the road, dustless, and wondered how many more miles was left in it.

About the time I finished loading the firewood, Pop throwed a piece on top, then settled behind the steering wheel and tossed his gloves on the dashboard. He raced the engine, and I climbed in. The sweat on my back felt cool as I leaned against the seat.

Pop eyed me. "Where the hell you goin'?"

"With you."

He sniffed. "Why you so helpful all of a sudden?"

I told him the ride would give me a break.

"Break? You ain't done hardly nothin'." He wedged his flask under the seat. "Chop the rest of that wood, then get your ass to work."

I squinted at him. Pop never turned down help. I couldn't say nothing about Savannah or beg to go with him, but I couldn't figure out why he didn't want me tagging along. I slid from the cab and slammed the door. He didn't even glance my way. He just pulled off.

I flung my shirt on the ground, then grabbed the axe and swung. The blade stuck in the log. I pried it free and took another swing. I was sick of Pop acting like he owned me—but he couldn't boss me around if I lived somewhere else. I recalled how Mamma's eyes had welled with tears when I had told her my plan. I had wondered if it was from me leaving or her realizing she would be alone with Pop. After she had gathered herself, she had said—when the time come—I could take her car and she and Pop would use Granny's.

I looked at the stack of unsplit wood, then at the knotted log in front of me. I grinned. Swinging with all my strength, I buried the blade deep in the wood, picked up my shirt, and headed to the sawmill to put in my notice.

Abigail IV

Flickers of Doubt

I watched my breath, knowing Donny hadn't added logs to the woodstove when he went hunting. He had crawled from bed before dawn, and I woke but had pretended to sleep. Now I was alone and cozy under the covers. I stretched my legs into the cold sheets, then curled up again in the warm spot.

I was reminded of snow days when I was a little girl and how I would awaken to the bright window and leap from bed and see the smooth, white ground. Knowing school would be closed, I would slide back beneath the blankets, excited to play in the snow but not ready to leave my soft bed.

The windows weren't bright today, but I would enjoy the quiet until Jesse started watching cartoons. Next year he would be a teenager, and I wondered at what point I would feel old based on his age. I knew I was too young to feel old now, but sometimes, when exhausted from life with Donny, I had a taste of it, and I needed mornings like this one to recharge.

How different our relationship had become from when I had wanted to spend all my time with him. I often thought about those early days with Donny and how they had slipped away so quickly. I had felt trapped in my parents' house, living with their rules, and I had considered them fogies who made everything fun seem like sin.

Donny had helped me let my hair down, and memories from my new experiences with him remained fresh. But when I became pregnant with Jesse, we settled into routine. Our relationship changed, Donny changed, and I supposed I changed. Going from carefree to parenting was too much for Donny. He seemed angry with me for getting pregnant and, later, angry at Jesse for being born.

With a baby in my arms, I struggled to finish daily chores, or "woman's work" as Donny called it—washing dishes, cleaning the house, folding laundry—and I couldn't imagine caring for a second child while Jesse was still a toddler, especially in a situation where I felt like I was on my own. If not for Mother's frequent visits, I would have been overwhelmed.

Avoiding Mother and reality, Donny worked late or stayed outside. On weekends, he disappeared for entire days. I didn't have the energy to fight him about it since I was up throughout the night feeding and tending to Jesse. My lack of sleep made most of Jesse's first year a blur, but one event was vivid, and I recalled Donny sitting across the room from me—a prisoner planning his escape.

"Missin' a card game," he had said, fingers splayed on his knees, head cocked to the side.

"We can't afford to give away money." I sat on the couch, cradling Jesse.

"It's only penny poker with some buddies. Fred, Murry, Billy Tucker." He shifted. "Cobble."

I knew Fred and Murry from the garage, but I hadn't met the other men. Jesse started crying. I bounced him on my knees as Donny watched.

"If you'd rather be somewhere else, don't let us stop you."

"I ain't played since Jesse was born." He scratched his whiskers. "Besides, Billy Tucker has connections with carpenters. I could moonlight for cash."

The phone rang. Donny stood, but he walked in the opposite direction. Jesse bawled. After the third ring, I said, "Will you please get that?".

He returned to the room and glared at me for two more rings, then answered. "Yeah." He held the receiver toward me as though I had a third hand. "It's Beulah."

"Tell Mother I'll call later."

Donny said, "She'll call you back", and hung up. He put on his hat, and I realized he had gone for it when the phone was ringing.

"You're a real piece of work."

"You want extra money or not?"

Jesse screamed, and I pressed him to my chest. "Just go!"

As Jesse calmed, I had flickers of doubt as to why I had been dead set on telling Donny the truth, and I couldn't help but think how different life would be if I had taken Mother's advice. In the heat of the moment when Donny had left to play cards, I had wished I had chosen Jefferey, but as my anger subsided and Jesse fell asleep, my clear conscience allowed me to rest. Still, I suspected I would regret my decision every time I was mad at Donny, which wouldn't be fair to him.

Lying in bed that night, not knowing when Donny would return, I had remembered the day my parents learned I was pregnant and my surprise at how prepared they were to lie about the father. I could never decide if their willingness to compromise their beliefs said more about them or Donny.

Now, lying in that same bed, beneath warm blankets, I wondered what other times my parents had bent or broken the rules to meet their needs—and I wondered if I would ever break them to meet mine.

I heard Jesse walk down the hall. The television buzzed when he turned it on. I savored another minute, then pushed the covers back and wrapped my robe over my pajamas, tying the cloth belt around my waist.

"I'm cold," Jesse said, when I stepped in the living room. He was sitting on the floor, wearing one of Granny's old quilts like a shawl.

"Are you helpless?"

He nodded. "I'm f-f-frozen!"

The hinges creaked on the iron woodstove door when I swung it open. Only embers remained. "Run get some wood right quick."

"Where's Pop?" He turned from the television.

"Hunting."

Jesse smiled and sprang up, dropping the quilt. He hustled from the room, barefooted.

We kept cowhide gloves beside the woodstove, and I put them on and slid the tray from the lower compartment as Jesse laid a log on the floor. "We'll need more." He was off like a shot. "Leave the door open!" Heat rose from the coals as I walked to the backyard and poured them in the metal bucket. Ash kicked up in the cold wind.

When the fire stoked, I shut the heavy door and latched it. I dialed the fan to high. Jesse had settled in front of the television again, shivering under the quilt.

"You'd be warmer with socks!"

As coffee brewed, I stared out the kitchen window. The bare trees swayed. Why anyone would sit outside in this weather was beyond me, but I wouldn't complain, and I knew Jesse wouldn't either. The house was peaceful when Donny was gone, and I considered how we would be better off without him. But no sooner had it crossed my mind than the thought saddened me—both for us and Donny—and I regretted it.

I peeked in the living room. "What do you want for breakfast?"

"Flapjacks!"

"Please?"

"Please."

I mixed pancake batter and made syrup as the house slowly warmed.

After breakfast, Jesse asked if Evan could spend the night. I was glad. Not only was Evan a hoot, but Donny was more tolerable when Jesse had company. When we arrived at Evan's, he ran to the car and slid in the back seat. I got a whiff of smoke. Shannon stuck her head out the door and waved, a cigarette hanging from her lips. Evan visited us more than Jesse stayed with him, and it dawned on me Shannon's smoking may have been the reason.

Evan scooted forward and propped his elbows over the front seat. "Have you heard the one about pigs and cornbread, Mrs. Hartline?"

"No, I haven't."

"Me neither. But I hear it's funny!"

I looked at Evan and smiled. He was all teeth.

Usually in winter, the boys explored the woods, but the bitter wind kept them inside today. They built a wall with blocks and made a ramp in front of it, then jumped toy cars into it. After rebuilding the crumbled wall, they would do it again. All the jumps looked the same to me, but some received louder cheers than others.

As I stood next to the woodstove watching them play, I wondered how a brother or sister would have changed Jesse's life, and I knew under different circumstances I would have wanted more children. Or at least one more: a daughter.

Evan crashed a car into the blocks. The wall didn't budge, so he karate-chopped it with a loud "Heya!". The blocks scattered. Jesse laughed—a genuine belly-laugh—and I wished the house was this joyful with Donny in it.

*

We were watching television when I heard the truck. As Donny walked through the kitchen, Jesse stiffened and looked at me from the corner of his eye.

Donny stepped in the doorway, smiling ear to ear. "Go look in the truck."

Jesse and Evan scampered out while Donny put his gun in the closet. When they returned, Jesse said, "Eight points!".

"Goodness! How many does it take to win?" They couldn't tell whether or not I was joking.

"When did you shoot it, Mr. Hartline?"

"After sunset. I heard leaves rustle and waited for him to clear some branches, then clucked my tongue. He stopped and raised his head, so I got a clean shot." Donny seemed out of breath. "He left a spoor a drunk bloodhound could've tracked."

"Them antlers is thick," Evan said.

"Gonna mount it." He pointed to a spot on the wall. "Hang it right there."

I imagined the deer staring at me when I sat on the couch. "Maybe we should—"

Donny clapped his hands once. "Hot damn, my luck has changed!"

I couldn't recall Donny being this happy, and I didn't understand why killing an animal brought out this rare side of him.

"What about the meat?"

"I'll take it to Earle tomorrow."

"Not tonight?"

"It'll keep. Nearly froze my balls off today."

Evan and Jesse looked at each other and burst out laughing.

Later that night, when Donny was on the edge of the bed taking off his boots, I sat beside him. He cupped a heel and slid his foot out.

"I know what's on your mind," he said. The boot hit the floor with a thud. "But I ain't never killt no deer with a perfect rack."

I shuddered, but I didn't want to derail before starting. "Well, if it's that important to you . . ."

"A'ight then. It's settled." He removed his other boot, then looked at me and raised his eyebrows.

I cleared my throat. "Do you know what's important to me?"

"Cookin' me breakfast." His eyes wrinkled.

"I'm serious. I have a question for you."

His smile vanished, and he grunted and rested his forearms on his legs. As I spoke, he pressed his thumb in his palm.

I told him how pleasant tonight had been and how I had enjoyed watching his interaction with the boys—telling them about his hunt, kidding with them, doing card tricks.

"It's nice seeing Jesse relaxed around you."

"Ain't he always?"

"No. He fears you."

"Fears—or respects?"

"It's fear, Donny. And he'll end up hating you."

"Child's got to be disciplined."

"He's a good boy."

"Because I don't spare the rod!"

I could feel the moment slipping away, so I took a breath and softened my voice. "Your mood controls him. And"—the words caught in my throat—"it controls me." I rubbed my thighs and squeezed. "When the house is full of tension, he curls up inside himself."

"You keep pointin' fingers at me."

"I'm not pointing fingers. But I can't remember the last time we were all on the same side—until tonight. So my question is: How could we make every day like today?"

He worked his hands in silence.

"What if we start over? Maybe go on a few dates now and then." I leaned over and nudged him with my shoulder. "See if we can find that old spark."

Donny stared at his hands, running his thumb across his scar. He seemed to consider what I said.

For me, a burden had been lifted. I was relieved I had finally said my piece, and I felt silly for dreading it so long. I tilted my head, trying to catch his attention. "Donny?"

He sniffed, then looked at me sideways, squinting his near eye. "You on the rag or somethin'?"

Donny IV
In Too Deep

Over the next few days, whenever the girl weren't in the barn, I worked on the roof—pulling nails, ripping off bad sections of metal, and overlapping new sheets with old. I'd sometimes catch a glimpse of her looking from the upstairs window. Other times, her brothers would run around in the yard while she sat outside with her nose in a book, licking her finger and turning them pages.

But yesterday, after Jim and the boys had piled in the car and rambled down the road, the girl had snuck to see me a couple times. Without the brothers to distract Gladdis, them visits had been brief, but our luck had held.

So I was geared up today, especially when Jim and Gladdis dropped the girl and boys off after church and left. The three of them had changed clothes in a jiffy, and the screen door almost flung off its hinges as the brothers had darted out the back. They had raced toward the creek while the girl had poked along the cow path behind them, focused on the ground. She wore shorts.

Them boys was old enough to handle themself in a stream, so I figured she'd slip away, but she was sunning herself on that boulder now, one leg bent and her forearm covering her eyes. I was hammering a sheet of tin, and she must've knowed I was watching her whenever the banging stopped. But after nailing another section with her not moving a muscle, I climbed down the ladder and crossed the field. Her brothers played upstream, throwing rocks in a pool at the bend.

"Why ain't you in the barn?" I said. She cupped her hand for shade and cut her eyes at me. I told her I needed help holding something and grinned. She laid her head back, eyes closed.

"I can't come see you anymore."

"Do what?"

She sat up and rested her chin on her knees, wrapping her arms around her legs, squinting at the water. "I won't be in the barn anymore."

What she said and how she said it raised my hackles. I wanted to knock some sense into her. Suddenly, I got dizzy. "Who'd you tell?"

She didn't move.

I grabbed her arm and yanked. "Look at me, girl!"

"Don't touch me!" She tried to pull free, her mouth twisting as her eyes flickered over my shoulder, and I remembered we wasn't alone. I turned my head. Them boys stood watching. The older one held a rock at his side. Even from that distance, I could tell they was scared.

I let go of the girl but looked hard at her. She never flinched.

As I strode away, I decided she hadn't told nobody nothing, or Jim would've been waiting for me with that shotgun. But now I worried her brothers might jabber.

By the time I got on the roof, the girl was stretched back out on that boulder. The sun burnt down. Now and again, the hot metal popped. I slid a sheet over part of the hole, heat scorching my glove as I propped on one hand to drive nails. When the tin was secure, I watched the girl. I whacked the face of the claw hammer on a naked rafter, making a slanted, round dent in the wood. The blow echoed with a clap. Goddamn bitch, I thought, luring me to the creek one day, then ignoring me another. My stomach felt on fire. If them boys wasn't here, I thought, or if I could somehow make that girl— My mind went all over the place, and when my hands started shaking, I knowed I should leave.

I wrung the wheel and fishtailed onto the road. Near Wilson's Crook, I seen Jim and Gladdis headed toward me and jammed on the brakes, then moved to the ditch so they could pass. Jim waved. My window was down, and dust flew in the cab. I drove to the graveyard and parked beneath a stand of oaks, drinking whiskey and thinking how the girl had never glanced my way. But her brothers had. They had waded to the boulder and stood beside her, staring at me after I had climbed on the barn.

That night, laying in bed, I realized I had took too many chances and decided to steer clear of the Sumner's for a spell. I listened to Abigail breathe and pictured the girl, then wondered if them boys had stirred up trouble. I imagined them sitting at the dinner table, their eyes as wide as they was in the creek, blabbing how the devil had took hold of their sister. I hardly slept.

The next morning, I crawled out of bed before daybreak. I drunk black coffee as I wore a path on the kitchen floor, the wood creaking each time I stepped in front of the sink. I knowed I'd be smart to work at Fred's and let the dust settle at the Sumner's. I needed to catch up nohow. When I finished the coffee, I stopped at the counter and laid my hands flat, straddling the empty cup. It was stained nearly to the rim. Then that cup faded, and all I seen was the girl propped on her elbows, wound up and waiting, her red dress laying in folds around her hips.

The hell with it, I thought. The shit-fire hell with it. I filled my thermos, packed a lunch, and left before Abigail woke. Clouds had rolled in overnight, and dew wet the tips of my boots.

Both vehicles was parked at the Sumner house, and the upstairs curtain was shut. In the barn, I leaned against a support beam, sipping from the thermos lid and staring at the blanket spread on the hay. I half expected Jim to bust through the door.

The morning drug by. I hung my toolbelt on a sawhorse, then walked to the creek. After eating a sandwich and apple, I tossed the core in the water. It bobbed downstream. The creek seemed quiet and—with no sun reflecting off the ripples—dark. I sat with my back against the boulder.

Rumbling thunder roused me, and I couldn't tell how long I had snoozed. I stood and stretched. My legs felt stiff, and needles pricked my foot. I stomped it, then limped to the ladder and hauled up the last two sections of tin. The roof was cool. As I hammered, my eyes kept straying to the curtain.

Them clouds growed darker. I smelt rain.

I was fixing to slide the last sheet over the rafters when I seen that girl swing the pasture gate closed. I rubbed my whiskers and glanced at the house. Both vehicles was gone. Them butterflies tingled as I tracked her. When she paused at the base of the ladder, she raised her face toward me. She didn't smile—she just had a flat look in her eyes. She stepped inside. What the hell, I thought.

I gripped the side rail and had one foot on a rung when I heard a vehicle. I waited. The two-tone brown truck broke from the trees and stopped at the end of the driveway. The postman placed something in the mailbox, then throwed his hand up and drove around the curve, his dust drifting over the field.

I hurried down and went in the barn. The girl was on the blanket, and she hadn't bothered to bring no book. A chain hung from the door, and I wrapped it around the bent nail on the doorframe and slid a loop on its head. I turned and watched her for a minute, then unfastened my toolbelt, letting it fall to the dirt. I heard nails spill. "Thought you wasn't comin' back." Thunder cracked on the heels of a flash.

As I walked toward the girl, a few drops spattered the tin, then the clouds opened up. The rain fell hard, pounding the metal, and you couldn't hear nothing over the racket. It blowed through the gap between the rafters, and water run down the wall, saturating the wood. The deep stain slowly seeped along the boards. After a while, the storm passed and the rain slacked, but it fell steady most of the afternoon.

The morning was clear and muggy. The shadows reaching across the yard shortened as the sun burnt off the dew. I stood on the porch eating breakfast, looking toward the shed. The other day I had asked Jim if he wanted a cord of firewood so it could cure before winter, and I had told Jesse to have it split. I'd stretch them loads until I thought of another chore to keep me near that girl.

The screen door shut behind me, and in the kitchen, I laid my plate in the sink. Jesse slouched at the table.

"Them logs won't load themself."

He didn't say nothing—just stood and walked out, the way it orta be.

Abigail give me a dirty look. "You could be nicer."

"Yeah. Meaner too." I knowed she was going to give me lip when she sat up straight.

"I'm sure he's glad you stay gone all day, treating him like you do."

"Him—or you?" She didn't blink. "Besides," I said, and grinned, "them bills won't pay themself."

She stomped from the room, her mug sitting in a brown puddle where she had slammed it on the table. I filled my flask with the last of the whiskey and made a pot of coffee. As it brewed, I heard Abigail getting ready for work, and I stared out the window above the sink, thinking about the girl's tangled hair, clutched in my fists.

At the truck, I set my thermos on the bench seat, then chucked some logs in the back. I climbed in the cab and cranked her. I was putting it in gear when the passenger door opened and Jesse hopped in. "Where you think you're goin'?"

"With you."

I eyed him. He never offered to do nothing. I asked why he was so helpful all of a sudden.

He shrugged. "Need a break."

Now that boy could split firewood for hours without showing no signs of tiring. He growed stronger each year and swung the axe and sledgehammer like they was nothing. "What the hell you need a break for?"

He looked sideways at me, prob'ly figuring I aimed to get drunk, which was fine by me. I glared at him until he got out. The door rung my ears. Christ Almighty, I thought. As I eased onto the road, I seen his reflection in the rearview. He had took off his shirt and was already chopping wood again, his back muscles flexing.

At the Sumner's, I locked the gate behind the truck and parked in the pasture. Old Red watched. His shoulder twitched, and a horsefly circled and landed. Then, one hoof scraped the ground, and I bet he'd've charged if that fence wasn't between us.

I found my toolbelt where I had left it, dusted it off, and put the nails in the pouch. It was still early for the girl, so I got on the barn and slid the last piece of tin over the hole and hammered it down. I walked the roof, adding nails here and there, then toted Jim's ladder inside and leaned it against the landing. When I went toward the sawhorses, I seen fresh marks on the ground next to the hay, and I took a closer look. The girl had wrote her name in the dirt. She had underlined it.

Then I noticed the folded blanket with the book laying on it. Daisy petals was sprinkled across the cover. I figured she'd come read soon, so I piddled away the morning and drunk coffee and studied her name etched on the ground. Something weren't right, but I couldn't put my finger on it.

I decided to unload the truck before the girl showed, so I drove to the woodshed in the backyard and watched the house as I worked. A downstairs curtain moved.

I had stacked half the logs when a thought struck me. I hustled to the barn then back across the field, scaling the gate again. After catching my breath, I rapped the front door with my knuckles. I raked my fingers through my hair, then knocked harder on the glass.

The door swung open. "I would appreciate it if you'd stop tracking mud on my porch!"

I glanced down but didn't see no mud. "Yes ma'am," I said, and tried to peek around Gladdis. "Is your granddaughter home?"

She crossed her arms and leveled her eyes at me. "The children left today."

I knowed them boys was children since they spooked so easy, but the sister was a she-devil. Then I felt a jolt, and my head went foggy.

"Is something the matter?"

That girl hadn't said nothing about leaving. She had hardly said nothing at all. The folded blanket come to mind.

"What's wrong with you?"

"Huh? Oh." I held out the book. "She left this in the barn."

Gladdis seemed less suspicious but still looked down her nose at me. "I see." She reached for the book and wiped it with her apron. When she turned it to dust the cover, we both must've noticed the title at the same time. Gladdis kept her head down but raised her eyes and met mine—like the girl had done in the creek, only Gladdis weren't smiling. I didn't know what it meant to her, but I had done a doubletake.

"Or maybe one of them boys had it," I said. But I had mentioned the girl first, and that tick was dug in too deep.

"No," she said, almost to herself, "they're too young."

I rubbed the side of my neck. "Well," I said, pointing, "you don't want somethin' that nice gettin' spoilt." I told her I was sorry to bother her and turned.

"Was she in the barn with you?"

I paused and looked over my shoulder and frowned, shaking my head. "I never seen her."

Gladdis didn't close the door until I was down the steps, and I felt her eyes drilling a hole in the back of my skull the whole time. I walked to the truck, opened the cab, and swiped under the seat. I took a long pull, then got the hell out of there.

As I bumped along the road, my thoughts slung every which way—Gladdis's beady eyes, the book, the girl. Finally, the fact the girl was gone weighed most on my mind. Gone without a goddamn word, I thought. Before she had appeared from nowhere, I had almost forgot what it was like. Abigail was always tired or had a headache or mad or on the rag, so I never got any. But now, after doing all them things with the girl, risking getting caught, and realizing it wouldn't never be that way again, my stomach burnt.

By the time I parked at Fred's, I was still mulling over the girl's name and the book's title. Odds was against them being the same. Then the idea struck me the girl might've hid a note somewhere in the book, and writing in the dirt was her way of telling me to look inside. That was why she left it on the blanket, I thought. And if a note was tucked between them pages, I wondered what Jim and Gladdis would learn if they found it before I did.

"Hey, old man!" Fred was standing beside my open window, and I jumped when I heard his voice.

"Best watch who you sneak up on."

He laughed. "You gonna sit out here all day?"

"Just puttin' off being around you bastards."

Fred laughed again. "Reckon you ain't got no choice. I told Cunningham we'd have his truck fixed this afternoon." He eyed the firewood. "Forget somethin'?"

"Nope. Itchin' to start on that truck."

Fred headed toward the garage. I called to him and asked if Jim had fueled up.

He stopped and turned. "First thang this mornin'. Them urchins was thowin' rocks at my sign. Durn near wrung their scrawny necks." He walked to the bay and ducked beneath the door. Murry clanged on something in the shop.

I looked down the road and took another slug. I'd need to search for that book soon. I didn't know if Jim planned to meet somebody or drive the distance hisself, but even if he come back directly, him and Gladdis would prob'ly attend Wednesday service tomorrow evening. If they got home while I was prowling through the house, I'd slip out the rear and be stacking wood when they seen me.

I finished the whiskey, then scratched my whiskers, staring out the windshield. The silo hadn't been used in years, and it showed signs of weather. I thought about how blades lose their edge, hinges rust shut, and hoses and tires dry rot—then something caught my eye. If I had ever seen it before, I never paid it no mind: A seed had took root on top of the silo, and a sapling had growed. I could barely see the thin trunk and little leaves outlined against the blue sky. I recalled them old oaks in the graveyard, and I wondered how big the tree would get until its weight collapsed the roof.

Jesse V

A Junkyard for Wrecked Women

I waited for a burger and fries at Milton's. I had never
been to a bar, and I knew it would upset Mamma even
though I had only ordered food. Several folks was eating at
tables, and a man and woman sat side-by-side in a booth.
One other person was sitting at the bar, and he slouched
over his drink except when he ordered another bourbon or
glanced at the door as it creaked open.

I had heard about Milton's from the lady at the motel
my first night in Birmingham. After I had rented a room and
tossed my suitcase on the bed, I had gone to snag change for
the vending machine. The lady had traded quarters for my
dollar, and we had chatted. She had rattled off places to eat
and said Milton's was her favorite. As I was saying
goodnight, she had reached in the drawer and laid my room
fee on the counter, pushing it toward me. I had told her I
didn't want to get her in trouble. "Sweetheart," she had said,
"where was you twenty years ago?" She had smiled, and I
could tell—in years past—she had been a beauty.

Before rolling out from the motel this morning, I went
to thank her again, but a fat man with greasy hair was sitting
at the counter, so I turned and left. I spent the day
searching addresses in phonebooks and driving to different
steel mills—most of them small and off the beaten path.
Usually the person in the office assumed I wanted a job and

would look confused when I asked for Evan Jones, but the woman at the large steel plant didn't miss a lick.

"This is a big place, hon," the woman said. "Maybe he works here, maybe he don't." She waved toward the door. "Feel free to look around." She picked up the phone receiver.

"Ain't you got no list?"

"If it's that important," she said, shuffling through papers and passing me a sheet, "we could use those strong arms."

I thought she was teasing at first, then I took the application. "How much you pay?"

She gave me the once-over. "More'n you make now."

I stepped from the office as she dialed the phone. The air stunk, and the brick walls was coated in soot. The windows was so dirty I couldn't see through them. One section had open bays, and sparks sprayed and ricocheted off men wearing heavy clothing and helmets. They must've been sweltering. The welder set his torch on the ground, pushed up his mask, and turned toward me. I couldn't tell if he was black or white.

I moseyed along. I heard the clang and hum of metal and machinery, and I seen coal cars from a train at the end of the long building lined with smokestacks. Them chimneys had looked skinny from far off, but once I stood beneath them, they made that silo behind Fred's seem like nothing. They spewed thick smoke. I recalled Evan's comment about them smokestacks, and I wondered if he had changed his mind about working here. Then I wondered if he had made it here at all.

While I considered what to do, a horn blowed, and a bunch of men come from one of the buildings and headed to the parking lot. Most of them moved slow, toward vehicles no better than mine, and their faces and clothes was dirty. I thought about how grimy my hands got when I tinkered with car engines and how hard it was to scrub them clean.

I stopped one man and asked if he knew Evan Jones. His eyes was glassed over, and he stared through me. I stepped aside.

I figured Evan hadn't found no fortune in that steel plant, and I didn't want no part of being cooped up in a furnace all day. I returned to the office, pulled the folded paper from my pocket, and slipped it under the door.

"Sure you don't want no beer?" the bartender at Milton's said, setting my plate down. The fries was piled high. I shook my head.

"Looks bad on me if you ain't drinking at my bar." He poured a beer and put it in front of me. "This one's on the house." He smiled, and I noticed his crooked teeth. Somehow, they reminded me of them old tombstones in the graveyard back home.

Staring at the full mug, I remembered how Evan would sneak his daddy's beer to Number 9 bridge. I had always took a sip or two. One time, after that game against Rogers, I drunk the whole beer—but I hadn't felt nothing from it. We would drop the empty cans in the creek and throw rocks at them as they floated downstream. I wasn't keen on littering, but we had fun sinking the cans. Still, Mamma would've tanned my hide if she had knowed.

When I was young, she had caught me tossing a bubblegum wrapper from the car window. She didn't say nothing at the time, but when we got home, she had told me to stay put. Then she come out of the house holding a bag and drove to where I had littered. "Find it," she said. From the car, old tires, white cups, and the occasional hubcap stood out, but I had never realized how much trash was in the ditches and edge of the woods since it was mostly covered with dirt or leaves. I finally found the wrapper and opened the car door. "Not until it's full," she said, so I lugged the bag, filling it with paper, cans, a shoe, a rusted lunchbox, and anything else that would fit. The gravel crunched and popped beneath the tires as Mamma inched along behind me. A few vehicles passed, and a man riding shotgun in a truck flung a bottle at my feet and hollered I had missed one. Both men laughed as they had sped away. Mamma watched the truck until it disappeared around the curve.

The bag was heavy before Mamma let me load it in the back. When I climbed in the car, she had looked me square in the eye, her finger in my face. "We are *not* white trash."

"Yes ma'am," I said. But I wondered how the neighbors would weigh in on that, and I knew she was fighting a losing battle with Pop.

The first time Pop throwed trash from the car after I had cleaned the ditch, I expected Mamma to scold him. I had sat in the back seat, looking from one to the other, but they stared straight ahead. After that, whenever Pop littered, it was always the same—Pop would grin, and Mamma's face would turn red.

"Need training wheels?" A guy with a ballcap and thin mustache had sat beside me, pointing at my beer. He reminded me of Evan, but smaller. I had eaten half my burger but hadn't touched my drink. The glass was sweating.

He ordered a beer and held his mug toward mine until I tapped it. "Cheers," he said. I sipped my beer, but he drunk about half of his. "You can do better'n 'at," he said. I took a big swaller.

"Name's Johnny." We shook hands, and he ordered another drink for both of us.

The bartender cleared my plate after I ate the burger, and I started my second beer. I waved off the cigarette Johnny offered. He shrugged. "My old man? He was buyin' me cigarettes when I was thirteen year old. Reckon he got tired of me filchin' his." He lit the cigarette. "Where you from?"

I eyed Johnny. "Puddin' Ridge, near Ider." I decided to finish my drink and skedaddle.

He took a drag and blowed smoke. "Never heard of it." He fidgeted with his lighter and looked at me sideways. "Figured you was from the other side of the tracks."

I fingered the handle of my mug.

He asked what had brung me to town, and I said I was searching for work. We talked off and on as we drunk. I learned he had lived in Birmingham his whole life, had quit his factory job three times, and had been recruited by a minor league baseball team before blowing out his elbow.

When our beers was gone, I told the bartender I wanted to buy a round for Johnny and pulled out my wallet to square up.

"Who?" the bartender said.

Johnny laughed. "C'mon, Seth. You ain't cuttin' me off already?"

Seth opened his mouth, then closed it. "Just busting your chops," he said, showing off them teeth. He poured two beers. I had only intended for him to bring one for Johnny, but there I sat with another beer in front of me. I shoved my wallet in my pocket.

"Ever drink a boilermaker?"

Next thing I knew Johnny dropped a shot of whiskey in our beers. "Now chug," he said. After a few seconds, he slammed his mug on the bar. The shot glass clattered.

I tilted my mug, tasting whiskey mixed with beer. I wasn't as fast as Johnny, and I spilled some—but I finished. He slapped me on the back and laughed again. Seth brung more beer.

The man who had been slouching over his drinks stumbled toward us, holding his glass. He laid his free hand on my shoulder and leaned into Johnny, like we was buddies. His head wobbled as he struggled to put his words together. "This here place," he finally said, slurring, "is a junkyard for wrecked women." Then he stood up straight, swayed, and downed his bourbon. "And I'm the tow truck." Me and Johnny didn't say nothing. "The tow truck," he said again. We kept staring at him. He slid the glass across the bar and staggered to a table with two women.

Johnny elbowed me and motioned with his thumb. "Been there," he said, and grinned. I didn't know if he meant the drunkenness or the women.

As I watched the man, I noticed the booths and tables was full. Cigarette smoke floated in blue-white waves along the ceiling. A young couple bent toward the jukebox, the girl pressing her finger against the glass. Music started playing, blending with the chatter. Near the center of the room, several people was shooting pool. One fella sawed his cue back and forth over the edge of the table, then thrust it forward. I heard a sharp smack. The balls scattered.

I realized the drunk man from the bar wasn't too far off the mark. Most of the women looked rough, and the two he had joined tried to hide it with makeup and overdone hair, but even through the smoke, their eyes looked as empty as their shot glasses. But I didn't see no high-caliber men neither—just a fair sample of tow trucks cruising around for beat-up or broken-down cars. I wondered how many of them folks had families needing the money they wasted on cigarettes and alcohol, and it wasn't no stretch of the imagination to picture Pop at a joint like this.

Then I remembered the woman who had given me the application and how she had made up her mind about me at a glance. I swung toward the bar and took a gulp.

"That's bullshit!" someone yelled.

The barroom got quiet, and it sounded like the music had been turned up. The fella who had broke the rack stood nose-to-nose with another man beside the pool table. Finally, the other man flung his cue. It hit a few balls, and they rolled across the table as he walked away. A ball dropped in a pocket, and I heard it land and roll down the chute. "That's what I thought," the fella said. His girl hung her arm around his neck. He stuck a cigarette in his mouth, and she reached with her other hand and lit it for him. Everybody went back to what they was doing. The music faded.

I thought of Pop again. "Ever any fights?"

"Used to have a lot," Johnny said, dabbing his cigarette in the ashtray. "That guy in the corner?" He nodded toward the last booth, and I seen a big ole boy sitting alone with a pitcher of beer. "Here ever' night. Don't pay for nothin'. Somebody starts trouble? He takes 'em out back."

"Then what?"

"Never been took out back." He grinned and lit another cigarette. He flicked his lighter on the bar and watched it spin.

I looked at the big boy in the booth again. He was probably twice my size. A pretty waitress stopped to talk to him, then laughed at something he said. When she turned away from him, he smacked her rear. She snapped her head toward him, but she was smiling as she walked off.

When I stood to find the bathroom, the alcohol hit me all at once, and the floor seemed tilted. I realized I needed to sober up before leaving, but when I returned to the bar, Johnny had ordered more beer, so we drunk and talked sports and then had another round.

The bright morning sun woke me. I squinted and squeezed my temples between my fingertips and thumb. The bartender's crooked teeth come to mind. And drinking at the bar. Then, only images—playing pool, sitting at a table with Johnny and a couple of girls, my arms grabbed from behind.

I jerked my head up. I was parked beside a grocery store. The keys dangled from the ignition, but I didn't remember driving. My clothes reeked of cigarette smoke. I scooted out of the car to get a clean shirt from the trunk, and I set my hand on the roof to steady myself. Sweat beaded on my forearm. After a minute, I walked behind the car and turned the key in the lock. The trunk lid popped open, and everything started spinning, like when I had stepped off the barstool. I wondered if I had left the suitcase at the motel, but then a thought struck me, and I reached for my wallet. That son of a bitch, I thought.

I mashed the lid closed and run my fingers through my hair. None of the buildings looked familiar. I sat in the car, slammed the door, and yelled. An old lady on the walkway scrunched up her face at me, then shuffled inside. I stared at the brick wall, gripping the steering wheel. The paint was flaking, and patches of red showed behind the white letters of the store's name.

I decided to find Milton's, wait for Johnny, and beat the tar out of him. But then I recalled what he had said about that boy who handled trouble, and for all I knew, he was the one who had throwed me out. The bartender might've been in on it too, the way he kept flashing them teeth and serving drinks.

Suddenly, my stomach turned, and I fumbled for the door handle.

I opened my eyes to a man with a nametag tapping his knuckles on my windshield, standing to the side of where I had been sick. He held his face close to the glass. His part was so perfect it looked like a bullet had grazed his scalp. "You need to leave," Davey said, his voice muffled. He stepped back and crossed his arms over his tie.

Davey was right, and without food, clothes, or wallet, I only had one place to go. Mamma would be thrilled, but Pop would laugh and poke fun at me. I cranked down the window.

"Leave, or I'll call the police."

I had considered calling the police myself, but I figured city cops had bigger fish to fry. I cleared my throat and wished I had chewing gum. "How far to the freeway?" My voice was hoarse.

Davey's expression didn't change. "Two miles," he said, then strode toward the store.

I seen streets going several directions. "Which way?"

Without turning, he pointed past the drycleaners.

I stopped at a filling station beside 59 and drunk from the bathroom faucet, then run cold water over my head. I dried my face with the front of my shirt. It smelled like bad decisions.

On my way out, them candy bars by the register made my stomach growl, and I glanced at the woman behind the counter. Near the door, I noticed roadmaps on a shelf. I paused. If I went home with my tail tucked between my legs, Pop would never let me live it down. I opened a map of Alabama, trying to remember the name of the place I had visited with my folks. I finally recognized the town and traced roads from Birmingham to Cullman, guessing the mileage. I had only met him once, but I reckoned Conley McBryar would hire me if I showed up at his sawmill. Pop didn't like Conley none, but Mamma said he had always been good to her.

"You buying that map, sonny?"

When I shook my head, water dripped from my hair, and a few drops landed on the map and soaked in. The woman pursed her lips, holding out her hand, and I stepped toward her. The map rattled as she found the creases and started folding. She kept her eyes trained on me.

I was still piecing together what had happened the night before, and one of Johnny's comments had stuck with me. I asked the woman what it meant if somebody said you was from the other side of the tracks.

She laid the folded roadmap on the counter and gave me a blank stare. "That all depends on what side of the tracks you live on, now don't it?" She never blinked.

The phone rung. She answered, scribbling on a notepad, then turned her back to me when she spoke. I glanced at them candy bars again. Her back was still toward me.

I walked out the door, wishing I could afford the map and thinking how the candy had been there for the taking. I grinned and slid my hand from my pocket. The keys jingled. When I fired up the engine, I recalculated the distance to Cullman, then looked at the dashboard. The fuel gauge showed half a tank, and I was afraid I'd lay up short. I whipped the car around and decided to leave a souvenir for Birmingham. Them tires squalled from the parking lot to the road.

Abigail V

Standing in the Dust

"Why does he think it was me?"

"He said you was lookin' right at him, Abigail!"

I thought about the expression on Murry's face as I had dumped trash on his porch yesterday. When I had seen him at the window, I had glared at him, grabbed the bottom of the open bag, and lifted. All the trash Jesse had collected from the side of the road spilled onto Murry's doormat. At the car, I had turned to see him stumble over the clutter as he came from the house, a few empty bottles bouncing down the steps. One broke. I had smiled as I had pulled away.

But, now, as Donny drove Jesse and me home, I didn't want Jesse to know what I had done. "Let's discuss this later."

"It weren't even Murry that throwed it out! He said Lyle done it."

"Well, I don't know where Lyle lives, Donny!"

"How do you think this looks on me, huh?" He banged the steering wheel with his palm. "Goddammit, what is wrong with you?"

"Don't curse around Jesse!" I glanced back. Jesse sat behind Donny, staring out the window, but I knew he took in every word.

Donny slowed to a stop. He jammed the gearshift in park, then twisted toward me, propping his elbow on top of the seat. "Tell me what to do again."

"Can we please go home?"

"First, swear you'll bury the hatchet with Murry."

"I will not! He threw a bottle at our son!"

"Goddammit, Abigail, that's a lie, and you know it!"

"Stop saying that word!" I realized I was pointing my finger at him.

Donny ran his hand the length of his face, and suddenly he seemed calm. "Get out."

I lowered my voice. "Don't make a scene. Not in front of Jesse."

Donny sniffed. "That's up to you now, ain't it?"

"So help me God, Donny." I stared ahead, gritting my teeth, fingers digging in my thighs.

Donny let the car idle and stepped in the road. In the side mirror, I watched him stroll from behind the car, thumbs hooked in his pockets. He spat, then reached out. Quick as thought, I whipped my elbow up, locking the door.

"Abigail." Donny yanked the handle. "Abigail!"

I slid to the driver side, slammed his door, and pressed the pedal to the floorboard, pelting him with dirt and gravel. In the rearview mirror, I saw him shielding his face with his arms. As I drove off, his yells faded. He pumped his fist in the air, clouded with dust.

At Tammy Weldon's house, I left Jesse in the car and knocked on the door. I heard the pitter-patter of little feet, then the longer stride of an adult. Tammy opened the door.

"Is this a bad time?" I could tell she was surprised to see me.

"Is everything okay?"

My eyes burned. I had never said "No" to that question before.

When I told her what had happened, at first, she had a similar expression as Murry when all the trash had scattered on his doorstep. Then her eyes crinkled.

"You left him there?"

I nodded, thinking about the times Donny had kicked me out of the car. Then I got tickled too.

"I bet he was madder than a hornet!"

She invited us inside, and I went and told Jesse. I rested my hand on the back of his neck as we walked in the house. Tammy asked her son to find some toys, and Jesse settled on the couch in the living room.

In the kitchen, Tammy brewed coffee, and I sat at the table. I asked how everybody was doing and noticed Katheryn peeking around the corner from the hallway. "Hi, honey," I said, and waved. She vanished. "She's cute as a button!"

"She has her moments," Tammy said, opening the cupboard. Two mugs tapped as she looped her finger through the handles. "But everyone's fine. Darrell works too much, but he comes to David's games, Katheryn's recitals, and PTO meetings, so I can't complain." She laid the mugs and spoons on a placemat. "His hair is thinning, and he hates it. Says it makes him look old."

"When I see him at church, I'll mention how he favors George McCullough from behind."

"Don't you dare!"

Tammy filled our mugs and set the pot on the warming plate. She placed sugar and cream in front of me, then sat in a chair, crossing her arms on the table and leaning forward.

I stirred the coffee and watched the steam and decided to tell Tammy everything: How Donny had left me on the side of the road several times over the years, how he sometimes knocked me around and threatened Jesse, and how he stayed out late without warning, staggering through the door at all hours of the night, usually with empty pockets.

I had bottled up my private life for years, so as I spoke, I felt the relief and exhaustion that comes from confession. Then it dawned on me: The last time I had told anyone about Donny was the first time he had left me standing in the dust. Since then, I had thought I was strong enough to handle everything myself—wearing smiles at church and work, around friends, and especially in front of Jesse. Even after Donny slammed me against the wall one night with his fingers gripping my throat, I had managed to fake a smile when I had tucked Jesse in bed a few minutes later, smoothing the covers under his chin.

"Is Pop mad at me?"

"No, baby. He had a bad day."

"What was that noise?"

"I fell over the footstool."

"Did Pop make you fall?"

"I tripped on my own."

I had sat with him until his breathing had slowed. Later that night, I had awakened, laying on the edge of Jesse's bed. I had dreamed Donny was choking me, pinning me to the wall. He had tobacco between his teeth and whiskey on his breath, and he had grinned while I gasped for air, my toes feeling for the floor. I had stayed with Jesse all night.

At the time, I had thought I told Jesse a lie, but now I knew I *had* tripped on my own—almost fifteen years ago. And as I shared events from my life with Tammy, I realized I had been falling ever since. At various periods with Donny, I didn't think I could sink any lower, but I wouldn't know I had hit rock bottom, truly, until I had started my ascent—if that day ever came. Then the image of Donny shaking his fist in the middle of the road flickered in my mind, and I thought perhaps today was that day.

I told Tammy story after story. It was different from talking to Donny. Whenever I voiced frustrations with him, he tried to fix everything. I recalled complaining about Joe scheduling me on a day I had requested off from the diner.

"You playin' hooky?"

"Of course not!"

"He'll take advantage of you until you stand up for yourself."

"I can't skip work."

"I don't know what to tell you, Abigail. If you got an itch, scratch it!"

I remembered staring at Donny, then leaving the room. He had heard what I had said, but he hadn't listened. I hadn't needed a solution—I had needed a shoulder.

But Tammy understood. She asked questions now and then and said "Land sakes!" after I described things Donny had done, but she mostly listened.

When I finished, Tammy told me she had known Donny and I had problems but hadn't realized the extent. She had struggled with whether or not to ask me about it, she said, and was glad I had opened up to her. Then she shook her head. "I can't imagine living that way."

"What choice do I have?"

We both knew one answer to that question, and we both knew I wouldn't leave my husband. It wasn't my vow to Donny making me feel trapped—I had made a vow to God. But even if I could somehow come to terms with breaking my word, I had seen the impact a broken home had on Donny. What if Jesse turned out the same and hated his stepfather if I remarried? What if Jesse resented me? If we divorced, would Donny move out, or would I need to find my own place? Would I have enough money for bills? What would people at church say? How would—

I took a deep breath. When I opened my eyes, Tammy came into focus. "It's overwhelming."

Tammy rested her hand on mine. "The Lord won't put on you more than you can bear." She patted my hand.

"Which is why he created coffee." Tammy stood and emptied the pot in our mugs.

I sipped, then heard a giggle. "Tell me about Katheryn's recitals." Tammy brightened, and between the caffeine and change in topic, my strength renewed.

The third time I called the house, Donny answered. I told him where I was and how I would only come home if he swore not to lay a finger on me. In the silence, I could almost hear him wondering what I had told Tammy—then he promised.

When we walked to the living room, Jesse was sitting on the floor beside Katheryn, playing with diecast cars. Katheryn cradled a doll. Jesse saw me and jumped to his feet. With both hands, he picked up a bigger car from the end table, then crept toward me, treating the toy like a cup of hot chocolate filled to the brim. He held it high.

"Look what David gave me!"

I eyed the toy, afraid Jesse had asked for it. I couldn't get a read on David, so I told Jesse to give it back. Jesse's shoulders dropped.

"Mamma said I couldn't keep it."

"Maybe you can build your own," David said, taking the car. "It'll look cooler than mine anyway."

We were saying goodbye when Katheryn handed Jesse something and ran away, her little feet pattering the floor. I watched Jesse unfold the piece of paper. Katheryn had colored a picture for him. It looked like a heart. I smiled at Tammy. "She's adorable! Can I take her with me?"

"Yes—the next time she throws a temper tantrum." We hugged. "You're welcome to stay here anytime. And that includes tonight if someone breaks his promise."

"I'm sure Donny would rather eat than argue tonight."

"Oh, Lord! Darrell will be here any minute, and he's probably expecting supper."

"Perhaps one day they'll learn to feed themselves."

Driving home, recalling everything I had told Tammy, I worried I had been unfair to Donny. I had only discussed the negative. It outweighed the positive, but I had tilted the scales, and Tammy's view of him would always be skewed.

I glanced at Jesse and noticed the folded paper in his hand. When I asked if he had fun, he shrugged. He was sulking, and—considering how his day had gone—I regretted not letting him keep the toy.

Donny V

Long Shadows

"*Lolita*?" Abigail's nose wrinkled. "Who was asking about *Lolita*?"

I lowered my eyes. The yellow from the fried eggs was spread thin where I had sopped up some of it with toast. "One of the guys at the garage."

"Did you boys start a book club?"

Abigail's lips went tight, and I wanted to slap that smirk off her face. "Just forget it." I pushed from the table and stood. "Where's Jesse?"

"Probably getting ready for work." She laid my plate in the sink. I looked hard at her, but I couldn't tell if she was sassing me.

"Well, the yard needs mowed." She cut off the faucet, still focused on the dishes. "You hear me?"

She stopped humming but didn't bother looking up. "I heard you."

I opened the door to walk out.

"She's an innocent little girl."

My heart jumped in my throat. Images of that girl come to mind: Leaning back in the hay and reading, holding down the board, sliding out of her dress in the loft. When I turned toward Abigail, the room started spinning, and I grabbed the doorjamb to steady myself. I had done that plenty of times, but never from feeling dizzy. As the spinning slowed, I seen Abigail scrubbing a plate. She had a watermark on her waist where she pressed against the countertop. I wondered if Gladdis had called.

Abigail looked at me sideways, setting down the dish. "What's gotten into you?"

"What girl?"

She sighed, then the floor creaked when she shifted. She put her wet hands on her hips. "What girl do you think, Donny?"

My knees almost buckled. I sunk my fingers deeper in that doorjamb and stared at Abigail.

"Lolita. Remember?" She reached for a towel, and I noticed her handprint on the side of her pants.

I didn't like her lip none, but onc't I realized she weren't talking about that girl, my legs firmed up beneath me. "I'll be sure to tell Fred." I knowed she watched me all the way out the door.

I sat in the truck and groped under the seat. My flask was empty, but no way in hell was I fetching more whiskey from the kitchen. I thought about how I had mistook Abigail, and I knowed I'd be looking over my shoulder until I found that book.

When I finished at the shop, I headed to the Sumner's with the firewood from the day before. Jim and Gladdis was home, but I still wagered on them attending Wednesday service, so I bought some time by pulling to the barn. I loaded them sawhorses between the wood and the cab and went through the barn to make sure I hadn't forgot nothing.

A sixteen-penny nail was laying on the ground. I picked it up, then walked to where <u>Lolita</u> was wrote in the dirt. Dust covered my boots as I shuffled my feet over the name. I studied the pile of hay, scraping my thumbnail across the gripper marks on the nail head. The blanket was gone.

Them rusted hinges grated as I shut the door. I glanced at the house and seen both cars, then eyed the upstairs window. Nothing moved. I turned and crossed the field and stepped into the shade, where the evening sun cast long shadows from the trees scattered along the creekbank. I stopped at the boulder. It seemed a darker grey, and rain had pooled in the hollows on top. The creek was still muddy, but it weren't swolled over no more, and tall shoots of grass leaned downstream between me and the bend, where water swirled. I stood for a spell. The swuft current stirred the air, but the creek seemed quiet.

I kept an eye on the carport, and after a while, I seen the Sumners going up the drive. I throwed the nail in the murky water and watched the car round the curve as I headed to my truck. I figured I had at least an hour until they returned. I'd find that book and either rip out the page the girl wrote on or take the note.

When I parked at the woodpile, Jim's two bloodhounds come up and sniffed the tires. I petted them for a minute and wondered if they sensed anything different as they followed me to the house.

I opened the screen door, resting it against my hip as I bent close to the backdoor pane and took a gander through the gap between the curtains. I tried the knob. It was locked, but I knowed they hid a key under the flowerpot. I turned the key in the lock and replaced it. I remembered what Gladdis had said about tracking mud, so I slid my boots off, flopped them on the ground, and stepped inside. The curtains on the window swayed when I closed the door. The kitchen smelt like home-cooking, and a cast-iron skillet was laying on a towel spread next to the sink. A cat was sitting beside a bowl of milk, watching me with yellow eyes.

One side of the dinner table was covered with mail and a newspaper. Near a stamped envelope, a roll of cash was wrapped with a rubber band. I reached over and weighed the wad in my hand. When I set the money on the table, I seen the name on the envelope: Amy Milford. The envelope was sealed, so I held it toward the window. The words on the folded letter blended. I put it back.

The kitchen opened into the living area. I walked through the wide doorway and stood at the foot of the stairs. I smelt furniture polish. The banister, balusters, and staircase shined a rich black walnut, and I pictured that girl wearing a red dress and leading me to her room. Then I seen a shotgun propped in the corner where the lower steps met the wall.

The floor was tongue-and-groove hardwood, and a rug was in the middle of the room with a coffee table between the couch and a couple of chairs. Wildflowers fanned from a vase on the table, and I wondered if they was the ones the girl had picked in the field. I remembered her tucking a daisy behind her ear.

The Sumners had an open fireplace, and the chimney tapered to the ceiling. A thick mantel was mounted to the bricks and held a clock and several photographs. The clock ticked loud in the quiet house. In the front of the room, heavy drapes was drawed to each side of the window. I imagined Gladdis at the door, holding that book after I had left. She prob'ly would've turned and set it nearby. I looked at the chairs and couch again, then the table. Beside the flowers, the book peeked from beneath a few magazines.

I heard something and spun. The cat was licking its paw on the staircase. The tags on its collar tinkled. Goddamn cat, I thought. My ears pulsed—almost in time with the clock.

I strode to the table and snatched the book, skimming through pages. I didn't see nothing. Then I flipped to the cover: *For Whom the Bell Tolls*. I placed the book facedown, like I had found it, and slid the magazine over part of it. I scratched my whiskers and noticed something on the mantel. As I got closer, I realized it was a frame laid flat. I slanted it—that girl and her brothers stared at me. The girl looked young, but them butterflies still fluttered. One of the other photos was of Amy and a feller I didn't recognize. Amy weren't smiling, but she was as purty as ever. Another one was an old black-and-white of Jim and Gladdis holding hands beside a Model A. I couldn't understand what Jim had saw in Gladdis, and I wondered how Amy had turned out the way she done.

When I turned from the fireplace, a jolt went through me. Christ Almighty, I thought. Bookshelves lined the wall on both sides of the opening to the kitchen. They was chock-full.

I walked to a shelf. I knowed what the cover of that book looked like, but not the backbone. I tilted my head, scanning titles. The cat purred and rubbed against my leg. I nudged it away and decided to start from the top, so I inched along the row, all the way to the corner of the room. I bumped down to the next shelf, backing to the doorway. Most names and titles didn't mean nothing to me.

I was about halfway done with one section when I heard a car door—then another. I straightened up. Through the window, I seen Jim and Gladdis walking toward the porch. Jim's mouth was moving, and he was shaking his head.

I glanced at the slew of books I hadn't checked, then hustled to the kitchen and slid across the floor to a stop. I turned the lock on the knob and swung the door to, then heard them come in the front as I eased it shut. Them curtains swayed again. The screen door tapped the frame as I guided it closed, and I snagged my boots and hightailed it to the woodpile. I jerked them boots on and jammed my hands in work gloves, yanking each cuff. I grabbed a log and twisted toward the row of wood. The split pieces settled into place when I dropped the log on them. My heart pounded.

As I emptied the truck bed, I contemplated all them books. I could search for hours and never find the right one. In my hurry, I might've even passed it over, and for all I knowed, they had other bookcases in the house. I'd need to deliver more wood when Jim and Gladdis was gone for a while. Sunday morning was a safe bet, but I had figured the same thing about this evening. They had either forgot something or skipped service. If they had skipped, I wondered—

The screen door smacked, and I turned to see Jim striding toward me. I knowed he had been watching since I had just stacked the last log. One hound half raised, seen Jim, and laid back on its side. I shucked off my gloves and set them on the woodpile, the tan cowhide darker where sweat had soaked in. Jim stopped at the tailgate. His head was bare, and brown splotches covered his scalp beneath his thin, white hair.

He pulled out that wad of cash. "What do I owe you— for everything?"

I told him. He eyed me, then thumbed through the bills and peeled off several twenties. Didn't even put a dent in it, I thought, stuffing the money in my pocket.

Jim rolled the cash and snapped the rubber band around it. "I won't be needin' anything else."

"What about the rest of that cord?"

"Keep your wood. I won't need anything from you for a long time."

I knowed he smelt a rat, and I could tell from his voice and the way his eyes narrowed I should hatch a new plan. I stuck out my hand. "Well, I appreci—"

"Don't forget your gloves." He turned on his heel and went toward the house.

My lip curled. The Sumners had always thought they was better than everybody—even Amy—so now I was glad I had something on them, and all the things Jim didn't know about his granddaughter flashed through my mind.

On the way home, I wondered how much Jim would piece together. If it was like with Amy, he'd stay in the dark. But Amy hadn't left no note laying around, and I was convinced one was tucked amongst the pages of that book. Either they'd find it, or it would remain hid until the girl come back—or until I broke in again. Then I recalled that shotgun in the corner and the glare Jim give me when I brung up owing him firewood, and the significance of him not shaking my hand weren't lost on me.

Jesse VI

Played for Fools

Clouds covered the sky tonight, so I walked slow in the darkness and finally found the landmark, then skirted the clump of trees. When I topped the hill, the bullfrog croaks guided me, until, all at once, them frogs went silent. I stopped. The night before had been bright, and I had seen the reflection of the moon on the pond's surface, but now the water was black, and its edge blended with the bank. I turned and crossed the open ground toward the thatch of pines between Billie Sue's backyard and the golf course. I slipped through the trees and crouched beside the last one. The house was dark, and the outline of the deck disappeared in shadow.

I had hidden behind this same pine last night. The kitchen and living room lights had been on, and Billie Sue's mother had sat on the couch, flipping through a magazine. When Billie Sue had walked in the room, my body had felt a surge. As I had watched, I had thought about the only other girl I had kissed, shortly before graduation. Our class had gone on a field trip to Chickamauga Battlefield, and me and Allison Giles had moseyed around, reading plaques about the Civil War. She had held my hand and led me from the white tower to a cannon at the far side of the field, away from everyone. We had straddled the barrel and faced each other. I had glanced over her shoulder and seen cannons aimed toward us, and I had imagined the courage it must've took to charge while cannonballs and white smoke had shot across the battlefield, the explosions kicking up clods of dirt that thudded to the ground. When Allison come into focus again, she had the same look as Angie Dobbins on that hayride. I had leaned forward.

While I had remembered my first kiss, the lights in Billie Sue's house had gone out, and the deck had shone in the moonlight. The backdoor had finally opened, and a silhouette had glided down the stairs and across the yard and headed straight toward me. Billie Sue had a bundle tucked beneath one arm. I had stepped from behind the tree and followed her. Standing on her tiptoes, she had whispered how voices carried over the fairway, and when her lips had touched my ear, I had gotten goose bumps. Then she had spread the blanket on the grass. As we had laid on it, she had turned toward me and run her hand on my chest, and I had felt that surge again.

So now I hunkered behind the pine and waited for Billie Sue, eager to pick up where we had left off. Earlier, I could've swore the door had cracked open and I had seen somebody, but after a long time of not seeing or hearing nothing, I knew my eyes had played tricks on me.

I peered through the darkness.

My foot started tingling, so I stretched my legs and changed positions, propping against the trunk. I tapped my fingers on the bark.

Then I seen something. A dark figure had appeared from nowhere, and I could tell someone was on the stairs.

Billie Sue must've been making sure her parents was asleep before leaving the deck. I considered whistling to let her know I was near.

I had already been expecting to spend more evenings with Billie Sue, and as I strained my eyes at her, I thought about how Mamma had called and said she was visiting Cullman in a couple of weeks. I had been excited, but now I reckoned she would get in the way. By then, Billie Sue would be sneaking to my place, but we wouldn't be able to see each other with Mamma in town.

I realized I was biting the inside of my cheek as I stared at the silhouette. Ready to slip into the darkness with Billie Sue, I looked behind me. The closest trees was black, the boles blending in shadow. I took a knee and crossed my forearms over my thigh, grinding the toe of my shoe in the dirt.

To hell with it, I thought. I stood and stepped toward the house—then froze. I slid back to the pine and slowly laid flat, peeking around the base of the trunk. My blood pumped even harder. I watched, wondering if I had just imagined it. But after a minute, I seen the orange glow again. The silhouette shifted, and the glow faded as it floated from one end of the deck to the other. Then I caught a whiff of cigar smoke.

My heart hammered the ground.

The figure paced, and as it turned from the stairs, I got on my elbows and knees. The pine needles was soft and quiet as I inched backward, crawling to the next trunk, never taking my eyes from the deck. When the cherry lit up again, I eased to my feet and brushed debris off my elbows. Hunched over, I moved from tree to tree toward the grass. The glow flared when I reached the last pine, and I turned and bolted. I misjudged my footing and fell, but I jumped up and scampered across the fairway toward the pond.

I slowed, and when the croaking stopped, I stood still and listened for footsteps. My pulse throbbed. I doubled over, catching my breath, then stared at the black water and remembered how, last night, the moon's reflection had seemed both on the surface and deep inside the pool.

When I stepped from the pond, them bullfrogs tuned up to full song in unison. A light in the parking lot showed the way, and as I walked to my car, I wondered if Conley McBryar knew about me and Billie Sue or if his smoking on the deck had been a coincidence.

Conley and his wife, Nadine, had took me in when I arrived in Cullman, which meant a lot since I had rolled into town on fumes and with nothing but the shirt on my back. They had let me stay in a trailer near their sawmill. Conley's aunt had lived there until she had passed away, and they was tickled to have someone mind the property—so they didn't charge nothing.

When Nadine learned my stuff had been stolen, she had bought me clothes and told me to wait and repay her once I got back on my feet. But, later, she had refused my cash.

I had been in Cullman two months, working long hours for Conley. His father had started the company and still come to the mill every day, but Conley run the business now.

Mr. McBryar had sat in the office the first Friday I got paid. I had opened my paycheck and gone to tell Conley they had made a mistake. But before Conley could answer, Mr. McBryar had agreed, and he had pulled a fifty from his wallet, slapping it on the desk in front of me: "We pay folks what they's worth". Then he had said he appreciated a man who looked out for the company. He had told me how he had built the sawmill from scratch, using timber off his land, and he had pointed to the framed pictures on the wall. One of them showed a young Mr. McBryar guiding a log through a ripsaw, a curved pipe hanging from his mouth. While his father had spoke, Conley had leaned back with his fingers locked behind his head, chewing a cigar stub.

Now, after leaving the golf course and driving to the trailer, my adrenaline was still pumping when I climbed in bed. I considered how I could've lost both my job and home for fooling around with Billie Sue, and as I stared at the ceiling thinking about her soft, wet lips, I knew I'd risk that tradeoff again. Sometime later, when I finally felt myself drifting to sleep, the memories seemed more real—rubbing my hands up and down Billie Sue's thighs, her bra straps sliding from her shoulders, her naked body glowing in moonlight.

*

At the sawmill the next morning, Conley had bags beneath his eyes. I had dodged him after clocking in, but he had sent for me at lunch. Of all the times I had sat in his office, I had never found myself on the business end of his desk until now.

"Am I working you too hard, son?"

"No sir." I had barely slept in two nights and must've looked as wore out as he did.

"Know why I called you in here?"

The chair creaked. "No sir." Since moving to Cullman, I had become a cardplayer, gambling small money with coworkers twice a week, but it was all I could do to keep a poker face while bluffing Conley. I held my breath.

"You cost me good timber." He run his hand over the back of his neck, tilting his head one way and then the other.

I breathed again. "I culled them ruined boards—so you could dock my pay." Running the circular saw yesterday, I had kept glancing at the clock, distracted by everything me and Billie Sue had done the night before and geared up to lay with her again. By the time the whistle had blowed, I had a pile of scrap wood.

"Not the lumber I'm worried about. You know how Marty lost his fingers?"

I nodded.

"You cut off your hand, it would take Jesus Christ himself to convince your mama it wasn't my fault."

"Yes sir. I'll be more mindful."

He took a cigar from a box and bit off the end, then spat it in the trashcan beside his desk. "I also want to talk to you about Billie Sue."

I squeezed the sides of the seat. He rolled the cigar between his fingers and thumb while a sweat bead inched down my chest. I recalled how, on the golf course, I had turned tail and run, but sitting at his desk, I was forced to play the cards Conley dealt.

"We're family," he said, and leaned back.

My stomach jumped. Conley and Mamma was first cousins. Before coming to Cullman, I had only met him once—when me and Billie Sue was kids—so I had never considered them close kin.

"So I trust you," he finally said. "Billie Sue's seeing some boy on the sly."

I sat still. I figured he was testing me, hoping I'd show my hand. Sweat kept trickling down my chest.

"Tried to sneak out again last night. I know she's nineteen, but under my roof, you live by my rules."

"Yes sir." He had said "again", so he must've caught Billie Sue slipping in the house the first night we was together.

"I saw you with her at the company picnic."

I gripped that seat.

He reached for a small box of matches and tapped it on his desk. Them matchsticks rattled. "Did she mention a boy?"

As he slid the box open, I realized Conley was off the scent. I let go of the chair and took a deep breath. I squinted at a picture hanging behind him and scratched my chin. "No sir. She didn't say nothin' about no boy." My mind drifted to Billie Sue's smooth curves and her milky skin in the moonlight, and I wondered when I'd see her again.

"Well, it's been going on for a while now," he said. "If I ever catch the bastard, I'll beat hell out of him."

He struck a match. The flame pulled toward the cigar as he puffed, and the tip glowed orange for a second. He shook out the match, and as smoke filled the room, my jaw clinched, and I knew me and Conley had both been played for fools.

For the first time since sitting across from him, I looked my cousin dead in the eye. "I'd thump him too." I decided to fold my losing hand, so I stood and reached for the doorknob.

Conley said my name, and I turned. He held a new cigar toward me. "Keep your ears open."

I strode to the lumberyard and switched on the saw. I set the end of a board next to the spinning blade and guided it. The saw made a high pitch as the teeth ripped into the lumber and tore through the top of the board. I watched the blur. When I pushed too hard, the saw's tone changed, and I smelled burned wood. Sawdust sprayed.

Later, when the whistle blowed, I kept working—head down, fingers clear of the blade—catching up from yesterday and looking forward to Mamma's visit.

Abigail VI

As the Evening Fell

"You hardly spoke to Billie Sue." Jesse didn't look up. I craned my neck, trying to catch his eye. Nadine had given him a plate of fried chicken and mashed potatoes, and he put the leftovers in the refrigerator. "You should do things together."

"We done a lot when I first come to town."

"I bet she has a pretty friend you could meet."

"She's usually with her boyfriend."

"Boyfriend? She didn't mention him."

"Never does."

Jesse opened the trailer door, and I followed him outside. Two aluminum lawn chairs were propped against the front steps. He unfolded them in the yard, and we sat, looking over a small field.

Jesse had lived in Cullman three months, and we had just returned from Conley's house. Nadine had cooked, and as we had eaten dinner, I couldn't get over how much Billie Sue and Brody had grown. The last time I had seen them, she wore pigtails, and he was starting kindergarten. Now, she was a young woman, and he was twelve.

My chair wobbled on the uneven ground. I stood to readjust it. "Tell me about your adventures."

"Not much to tell."

"What did you do?"

"Went to Birmingham, seen steel factories, and come here."

"How did you decide on Cullman?"

"I remembered what Conley told me about that board I cut."

"That was years ago!"

The leaves had turned, and I watched several drifting over the field as they fell. I compared the bright colors of the tall trees in front of us to the dull green of the pines behind us, planted in rows.

When I was here last, the pine trees had been small, and Conley had mentioned how the sawmill had recently harvested that section of timber and replanted. We were headed to the grocery store when he had detoured down the road toward the trailer. I had been cooking with Nadine, and she had called Conley to the kitchen and asked him to run to the supermarket for bread. He had taken his keys from the hanger beside the door and was halfway out when he stopped and said, "Why don't you come with me?".

I knew Donny wouldn't like it if I went with Conley. Earlier that day at the family reunion, I could tell Donny was irritated when Conley and I had pitched horseshoes together. According to Donny, I had laughed too much. But I had pointed out how Nadine had laughed right along with me. Then Donny had gotten angry during the three-legged race. He claimed Conley had meant to fall, dragging me down on top of him. When I had reminded him we were cousins, his face had turned red. But as I had watched Donny fish for a beer in the cooler, I had felt a hint of guilt: I knew Conley had been flirting—innocent flirting—and I had liked the attention.

So when Conley asked me to ride to the store, I was tempted, but I hoped to avoid further friction with Donny. "I should stay and help Nadine."

"The hard part's done," she said. "I'll tell Donny for you."

With no other excuse for staying, I left with Conley. He poked through downtown, giving me a history lesson on Cullman. He knew the owner of every shop. As we passed the sawmill on the outskirts of town, he said his father planned to retire soon and hand the business over to him. Then he pulled down a sideroad near the mill and stopped. The car idled.

"Aunt Clair lives in that trailer." He lifted his chin toward the end of the dirt road. "Dad bought it for her, so she could move closer. He checks on her every day."

I made a comment about how thoughtful he was.

"To family and friends." He shook his head. "But don't get on his bad side."

He looked sideways at me, tapping his fingers on the steering wheel. Suddenly, my heart fluttered, and I wondered if he had wanted to show me where Aunt Clair lived—or be off the main road.

"Well, should we go before the store closes?" I laughed, but even I could hear it didn't sound natural.

He turned toward me, then reached and touched my hair, pushing it behind my ear. I considered brushing his hand aside, but then he rested it on the seat.

"I need to tell you something."

Images from the day rushed through my mind, and I feared Donny may have been right.

"You're a beautiful woman," he said. "Fun. Full of life."

My heart sank. "Conley, I—"

He raised his hand. "Let me finish."

Then he touched my knee. I tensed. I wanted his hand off me, but I was scared to do anything.

"Abby, . . ." He squeezed my thigh and released it. I felt my face flush. I couldn't believe he had put me in this position, and I didn't know how I would face Nadine when we returned.

His chest rose, then I heard his long exhale. "I don't like Donny," he finally said.

My lips parted.

"Had a few run-ins with men like him." He stopped fidgeting. "I can't explain it, but I've always felt close to you. We've been together—what—four, five times?"

I nodded.

He glanced out the windshield toward the pines. Then I saw a flash of anger when our eyes met. "Has he ever hurt you?"

His question caught me off guard, and I was unsure what to say. If I said "Yes", for all I knew, Conley would make a beeline to the house and confront Donny, but if I said "No", he would probably know I was lying.

"Things are better," I said. And things had been better, but they were still a far cry from good, and Conley seemed to sense it.

"I saw how he treated you today. Don't let him smother you." He patted my leg. "Know this: If he so much as gives you a cross look, call me. I'll come handle it."

My head was spinning, but everything slowly came into focus. Conley's touches, I realized, were just his way. I remembered how Father used to stroke my hair and kiss my forehead when he tucked me in bed and how comforting it had felt. I had a similar feeling now, and Conley seemed like an older brother protecting me.

He put the car in gear. "Let's get that bread."

As Conley drove toward the store, I was relieved I hadn't pushed his hand away, thinking he was getting fresh, and I was embarrassed Donny had convinced me Conley had anything other than my best interest in mind.

"There's the old mill." Conley pointed across the dashboard. The hair on his tan forearm was blonde. I looked in the direction he indicated, then kept staring out the window, dreading what would happen if he learned the truth about Donny.

After dinner, more relatives came to Conley and Nadine's house, and they stayed late, catching up and telling stories. Most everyone was pretty deep in liquor, and all the commotion was too much for Donny. If not for the alcohol, he would have been miserable. He only spoke if asked a question. But I laughed and carried on with everybody. Jesse went back and forth between playing with the other children in the next room and joining the adults. He would sit as close to Conley as possible.

People left at different times until it was just Conley, Nadine, and me, with Jesse asleep on the couch. At some point, Donny had slipped off to the guest bedroom.

"I didn't want to bring it up with others here," Nadine said, "but how's Jackie—really?"

"She and Dewayne seem great. But when they moved, they made it clear small-town life wasn't for them. They've only visited twice in five years. It hurts Mother's feelings—especially on holidays."

"They're only a few hours away," Nadine said.

"Jackie doesn't like spending her time off"—I looked at Jesse, and his breathing was easy, but I still whispered—"with everyone in the family."

Conley grunted.

I laughed. "Jackie's never been afraid to speak her mind, so she and Donny clash." I pushed Jesse's bangs across his brow. "But they've taken root in the city and have careers. I wouldn't like it—all the traffic, noise, and crime."

"Abby was always the smart one," Conley said. Then his tone turned serious. "They can live how they please, but they shouldn't abandon kin."

Nadine rolled her eyes but smiled. "Don't get him started. He'll stay on that soapbox all night."

Conley had promised to show Jesse the lumberyard, so the next day, on our way out of town, we visited the sawmill. Mr. McBryar was sitting behind his desk and told Conley to give us a tour. As we walked through the mill, Conley paused at each piece of equipment, explaining the stages of how logs become lumber.

We stopped at a large saw where a man stooped, slowly pushing a board. He didn't turn from the wood until he completed the cut. I noticed two of his fingers were nubs.

Conley asked Jesse if he wanted to run the saw, and as the man helped Jesse cut a board, I stared at his hand. I must have looked nervous because, over the buzz, Conley told me to relax. "Marty's my best operator."

I leaned closer. "What happened to his hand?"

Conley kept his voice raised. "Let's just say he hasn't drunk another drop. Losing his fingers saved his job—and marriage." Conley glanced at Donny, then walked to the saw and switched it off. The shrill faded as the blade spun to a stop.

Marty held up his hand, showing us his thumb, pinky, and crooked ring finger. "Cain't hold the bottle no more." He winked.

Sliding his palm along the edge, Conley studied the board. "By God, you can't cut cleaner than that." He tousled Jesse's hair. "Come work for me anytime."

Jesse stood tall. I tried to brush sawdust from his shirt, but he shrugged me off.

"We need to hit the road, Abigail."

The lumberyard had a gas pump, and Conley told Donny to pull next to it. Mr. McBryar stepped from the office. He removed the nozzle, stretching the hose around the car, and pumped gas. Donny climbed out and spoke to him, arms crossed.

When the tank was full, we huddled at the car, saying goodbye. I thanked Conley, and he gave me a bearhug. Then he shook Donny's hand. As Donny started to turn away, I could tell Conley tightened his grip. "You take care of her."

Donny squinted. "Always do."

I was afraid I would need to step between them, but they both let go, and Donny got in the car. I touched Conley's arm. "We should do this more often."

He nodded, but I saw concern on his face.

As we drove off, Jesse watched the mill from the rear window. He had sawdust in his hair. It was just the three of us again, and I wanted to relieve the tension since we were stuck in the car for a couple of hours—but I couldn't resist goading Donny once more. "That sure was nice of Conley, giving us gas."

Donny scowled. "His daddy give us the gas."

I held back a smile.

I hadn't mentioned Conley's name to Donny again until I told him where Jesse was living. Donny and I still hadn't discussed Jesse leaving home, and I had walked to the porch, thinking I would sit with him as the August evening cooled.

"Jesse called."

Donny planted his feet, stopping the swing.

"He's in Cullman. With Conley."

"The hell with Conley." He placed his bottle on the rail beside the swing. The chains creaked again. "Thought he went to Birmingham."

"He did."

"Why double back to Cullman?"

"I'm thankful he's with someone who cares about him."

Donny hadn't been abusive since the night I had shot the gun over his head—almost a year ago—but he had seemed on edge lately. I had assumed it was because of Jesse. But now—even though I hadn't intended to compare him to Conley—the look in Donny's eyes told me I was on thin ice, and as I went inside, it dawned on me: With Jesse gone, perhaps the rules had changed from Donny's perspective, and I wondered if the bullet I had fired had finally run its course.

Something broke my train of thought, and I was back with Jesse at Aunt Clair's trailer. The weather was mild for November, and the light jacket I wore had been warm enough at first, but I reached and pulled it close around my neck.

I looked at Jesse, but he remained quiet. Then I saw my old car parked beside Granny's Buick, and I thought about what had led us to this point in our lives—balanced in rickety chairs on a lawn in Cullman, sitting between the old trees with tangled branches and the young ones planted in rows.

On the day Jesse had left, I had ridden with him to Granny's house. Donny had been more upset about the car situation than Jesse leaving since he figured it would be short-lived.

"Won't be gone a week," Donny had said. "When his belly's empty, he'll come home. But you can't steal Granny's car."

"I didn't *steal* it. I talked to her, and she said we could borrow it."

"She won't remember that, and you know it."

"She can't drive it anyway."

"Because you stolt her keys!"

A month earlier, I had taken Granny's keys without her knowing. She had driven to church and ended up at Jefferey Smith's house, thinking it was hers. He had heard someone at his door and saw Granny trying to fit her key in his lock, so he had phoned. When I arrived, Granny was sitting in the passenger seat with her purse in her lap, fingers wrapped around the straps, staring straight ahead. I asked Jefferey if I could leave my car until Donny and I picked it up later, but he insisted on following me to Granny's.

After getting her settled, I slid Granny's car key from the ring and into my pocket, along with the spare. As I returned with Jefferey, I realized I should have driven my car to Granny's house first. I imagined the rumors if anyone saw it in his driveway—especially since he and his wife had recently separated. Jefferey had been a regular at the diner for years, and other waitresses had said he was sweet on me. I called them crazy. Still, it was fair to say I chatted with Jefferey more than any customer.

When Jefferey parked in his carport, he invited me inside—"Just to visit," he said. I declined. But we sat in his car and talked awhile. Whenever a vehicle passed, I glanced toward it.

He reached and placed his hand on top of mine. "You're not doing anything wrong."

I couldn't tell if the tingle was an invitation or warning, but I knew most people would disagree with him. I slid my hand from beneath his.

Donny and I hardly touched anymore, and I fulfilled my duties as a wife as little as possible. It never lasted long, and sometimes the dreading was worse than the act. But I still desired to be caressed—to have my neck rubbed, to feel fingertips glide across my skin.

Sitting in the car, I was reminded of that day with Conley. But unlike Conley, Jefferey had more than my best interest in mind. I wondered what Donny would think if he found out. Would he be angry? Jealous? Or would he even care?

I tried to make light of Jefferey touching me by holding up my hand and clicking my thumbnail against my ring. "Are you forgetting something?"

"Yes," he said, "my manners." He leaned toward me.

My head tapped the window when I pulled back. I gently pushed him away. "Jefferey. I can't."

He backed off. "But you wish you could, if Donny was out of the picture?"

"I need to go." As I stepped from his car, I realized my answer should have been "No". Jefferey had never been so bold as a teenager, and I wondered how else he had changed—and what changes he had noticed in me.

When I rolled down my window to thank him again, Jefferey said, "He's a cinderblock, Abby—on which all your hopes are stranded". My stomach felt hollow as I left.

I drove the backroads home, comparing my conversations between Donny and Jefferey. All Donny and I ever talked about was work or weather, and we usually ended up arguing and spending the evening avoiding one another. But Jefferey actually wanted to understand me, and he asked my opinion on every topic we discussed.

I thought about him trying to kiss me, and I could only guess how far it would have gone if I had leaned forward. I couldn't remember when Donny and I had last kissed—at least more than a peck. I had lost my passion for Donny long ago, but I supposed it was partially my fault since I had never forgiven him.

I didn't know what I felt for Jefferey—maybe it was temptation, or maybe I just liked attention—but since I had denied him, I had done nothing to regret.

*

As stars began to shine in the twilight, my mind lingered on Jefferey, and I recalled how—when a young girl—I had told Mother he was boring. Now I knew it was stability, rather than dullness, and I longed for that trait in Donny. Two months ago on our anniversary, Donny had come to the end of his rope. I remembered his anger, how I had slept in Jesse's empty bed, and how I had compared Jefferey's soft touch to Donny's coarse hand before finally falling asleep after a restless night of staring in the dark.

A movement caught my eye. "Since when do you smoke?"

"Conley gave it to me."

I heard a scrape, and a flame flared in the dusk. The smoke floated and disappeared.

"Remind me to ask him about that." But I couldn't even pretend to be mad at Conley. I was eternally grateful he had taken Jesse under his wing. "How do you like working for him?"

"Like it."

"And living on your own?"

"I have everything I need."

My mind drifted to the bare walls of the trailer and the lack of decorations—clear signs a man lived in it. I suddenly realized I had never thought of Jesse as a man before. When he was small, I could tend to his sniffles or skinned knees, but I was no longer sure how to comfort him. Then it dawned on me how, when about his age, I was pregnant. At the time, I had felt grown, but now I saw how young I had been—and how I had not fully understood what I was getting into.

"It's so peaceful here," I said, glad I had made the trip without Donny.

Jesse puffed his cigar. "I ain't walkin' on eggshells."

His words broke my heart, and my throat knotted. I recalled my decision to stay with Donny for the sake of the family and doing the right thing in the eyes of God, the church, and myself, and I considered it may have done more harm than good.

"Do you ever get lonely out here?"

"Sure don't."

"Scared?"

He turned toward me. "I'm gonna play like I didn't hear that."

I laughed. In the fading light, I couldn't see his face, but I knew the look he gave me. I asked other questions about the sawmill and Conley and Nadine, and as the evening fell, Jesse started talking more—more than I had ever heard him talk. I didn't know if it was the cigar or the darkness, or maybe he *had* been lonely, but his typical short answers expanded, and we had our first real conversation. It was one of the best nights of my life.

The next morning, we ate breakfast at Conley's house. Billie Sue slept in, but Brody sat beside Jesse before catching the school bus. I handed him his lunchbox as he hustled out the door. Watching him run to the bus—lunchbox banging against his leg—I was nearly brought to tears.

Nadine chased Jesse and Conley outside as I cleared the plates. She tied an apron around her waist and refused to let me help wash dishes. I relaxed at the table, savoring the last of my coffee.

"Jesse told me you and Conley treat him like one of your own."

"He *is* one of our own—and we're lucky he's here. Jesse's a hard worker. Plus, Brody sticks to him like glue."

"At least let me pay for his clothes."

She glanced over her shoulder. "Nonsense. I was bribing him for when Brody needs a sitter."

After Nadine dried the dishes, we all gathered beside the car. I hugged Nadine and Conley, thanking them. Conley warned not to speed in the small towns.

Jesse opened my door and said he hoped I drove the car better than Granny. Then his expression changed. "I won't make it Thanksgiving, but I'll be home for Christmas."

I squeezed him tight. A few weeks ago on the phone, he had said he was staying in Cullman for the holidays.

My heart full of joy, I headed home, thankful to God that Jesse was with family and not lost in Birmingham—working in a grimy factory with strangers, lowlifes like Johnny stealing from him—and I took comfort in knowing I would see him again soon.

Donny VI

Wildflowers

I waved toward the window. From my angle, I only seen reflections on the glass, but I knowed she sat in her chair, watching.

I picked up sticks from the storm and slung them in the woods, then walked to the shack behind the house and drug out the lawnmower and filled it with gas. I pulled off my boots and put on the old brogans I stored in the shack. My foot on the mower's deck, I yanked the cord. The motor purred. The ground was still damp from a midday shower, and even though it was September and the grass weren't as thick, it clogged the chute in wet chunks. When I finished, dark green clumps lined the yard in rows, and I toed the big piles, spreading them out. Should've made time to rake, I thought.

The mower rattled over uneven ground as I pushed it toward the shack. I swopped boots and carried the empty gas can to my truck, then went to the house and stood on the mat. Mrs. Buffington opened the door before I knocked.

"Hey, Donny!"

I wrung my hat. "I can't come in." I seen disappointment in her eyes. "It's our anniversary. Abigail reminded me yesterday. I'm sorry."

"Never apologize for doing right. I appreciate you tending my yard on such an important day."

"I'll visit a good long while next time. Promise."

She smiled. "That'll give me something to look forward to." Then her face changed. "He called."

She hadn't uttered them words in well-nigh six months.

"Where was he?"

"He didn't say, and I didn't ask."

"Wish I'd've been here."

"He's the last Buffington."

"Ain't dunnit. We still got you."

"Not for long."

"You don't know that. Besides, when it happens, you'll be up in Glory smiling down on the rest of us."

"It would do my old heart good if you actually believed that." We locked eyes, then I looked down. She walked away. When she come back, she held a brown bag, folded at the top. "Your favorite."

I smelt cookies. "I hate I can't stay."

"You should be with Abby."

"You need anything?"

She shook her head. "But expect a list on Thursday." She reached for my hand and squeezed it. Her skin was cool. "Take care of yourself."

"Always do."

She waited at the door, watching me drive off. I dug my hand in the bag and ate two cookies, then rolled the bag closed and shut it in the glovebox, next to my .45. I knowed a load was off Mrs. Buffington's mind since she had heard Marlon's voice.

I remembered when I had last seen him—during hunting season. He was passing through town, so I had laid out from work. We had hunted his property one day and Redbriar the next. The deer was in rut and a cold front had moved in, so I figured I'd at least draw a bead on one. Me and Marlon had put our tree stands within sight of each other, and I had saw a trophy buck forage below his stand, him just staring at it. I had smiled. Marlon weren't timid to pull a trigger, and I recalled the first time I had saw him watch a buck walk away. "I've killed men without regret or compunction," he had said, after I had asked about it, "but a deer what ain't wronged nobody—that's different." Marlon had said he had killt plenty of animals over the years, but he hadn't shot a deer for sport since hunting with his daddy. Them bucks never knowed how lucky they was.

I reckoned we both just liked being in the woods, away from it all. The only place I had peace and quiet was in a tree. No Abigail, no Jesse, no work, no nothing. Just me and wildlife. I learnt a lot by studying animals—they always got what they needed, and they always stayed alert.

Me and Marlon enjoyed scouting almost as much as hunting. Whenever we scouted a new area, we'd drive to the nearest town, searching for a bar. We'd drink and cut up with the waitresses, but every so often, when drunks seen the Ranger patch on Marlon's coat, they wanted to test him. Sometimes Marlon ignored them, but when they pried under his skin, it typically come to blows. I covered his back if other folks jumped in, and we usually won brawls, but one time we had fought off four or five men when a feller knocked me down with two licks I never seen coming. That feller would've won a clean fight, but when Marlon flashed the jagged end of a broken bottle at him, he cleared out. After the dust settled, the bartender told us the man had been an undefeated Golden Gloves boxer in the Navy.

"Ain't no glove gonna beat me with a bottle—no matter the color," Marlon had said. But we both knowed we was in over our head on that one, and it tore Marlon up to admit a sea dog had got the better of him.

But most of our evenings was tame, and after scouting or hunting, we'd sit around a fire. I'd open my hands to the heat and stare into them flames as Marlon told stories. He never told the same one twiced, and most of them was light in nature.

On our last hunt, he told me how two brothers had drawed pistols on each other over ten dollars when he was reffing chicken fights in their living room. Then he told me about siphoning gas from a waitress's car and walking out with her after she got off work. "My buddy's the mechanic," he had said when her car sputtered, "but I can give you a lift." She had invited him inside, and he thought his plan had worked—until her husband opened the door, gun in hand. Marlon hadn't flinched: "Take all that money I give her and buy a ring". He later learnt she tripled her tips when men thought she was single.

But now and again, Marlon would talk about the war. When he did, his eyes would glass over, and he'd stare at nothing. His tone would change, and he'd slip into a story about hiding within spitting distance of death, the night so dark he couldn't see his hand in front of his face, the enemy so close Marlon could smell him. Or he'd tell about one of his buddies shredded by a landmine, or about ripping out a soldier's jugular with his teeth as they was gripping each other's wrists in a knife fight.

All them memories was why he disappeared— sometimes to rehab, other times nobody knowed where. Mrs. Buffington didn't understand why he stayed gone, but Marlon had never told her what it meant to be in Special Forces.

The first time he had brung it up, I had asked if he was ever on a mission so hard he didn't think he'd make it back.

"They was all hard," he had said. "Why do you think they sent me?"

"You weren't never afeared of dying?"

He had leveled his eyes at me. "Fear is having something to lose."

Ever since that day at the liquor store when he had sported that new haircut, I had looked up to Marlon, but after I learnt what he had been through, I realized he was the toughest son of a bitch I knowed.

Onc't in a while, we'd talk about Mr. Buffington, but it burnt Marlon up not knowing who had killt his daddy, and Marlon always said he'd never rest easy until he had planted a bullet in that man's skull.

"If he'd lived, you'd be managing the store for him," Marlon had said on our last hunt. We was sitting beside a campfire. He flicked his cigarette butt in the hot coals. Marlon never smoked while hunting—he just chewed on a matchstick—so he'd make up for it later, and he had already plowed through half a pack. "But sellin' was the only option."

I nodded. No telling how many times I had thought about Mr. Buffington's death and the ways it had changed my life. I couldn't shake the image of him laying on the floor behind the counter, bleeding out and dying alone. "Reckon both our lives'd be different."

"You wouldn't be strapped for cash and workin' on barns."

I run my hand over my whiskers. "It weren't all bad."

"And you sure as hell wouldn't be in the hole to Cobble."

"At least he's lettin' me piss-chip away at it."

Marlon poked at the fire with a stick. Sparks flew. "What if he gets antsy?"

"He won't. He knows I'm good for it." But Cobble *had* gotten antsy, so we had struck a deal where I had been working on his house as payment, but that could only get me so far. If Abigail had caught wind of it, she'd've been ticked off about the money—but she'd've downright throwed a fit about the remodeling. She'd hounded me about our kitchen for years.

But even though I hated owing Cobble, I was more shook up about my rotten luck, and I had spent many a day ruminating on if I was snakebit not only in gambling, but in life.

Marlon tapped a pack of cigarettes against his palm, then dropped the wrapper in the fire. It shriveled in a blue flare. "Never liked Cobble." He lit a cigarette with the flame on the end of his stick, then blowed out smoke. "If he pushes, let me know."

I couldn't help but grin. "Got somethin' in mind?"

He held the stick close to his face, staring at the brand. "People have accidents. Even Cobble."

That comment was Marlon in a nutshell. No matter what I done—right or wrong—he always had my back.

But Marlon had been gone for almost a year, and now Jesse was gone. I had growed used to living without folks I cared for—Mr. Buffington was dead, Granny couldn't remember nothing, and the fun Abigail had disappeared long ago.

Still, I would've laid odds on tonight being different with Abigail since it was our anniversary. But I knowed I needed to get her something if I wanted a shot at getting anything from her.

So after leaving Mrs. Buffington's house and checking on Marlon's trailer, I stopped at the entrance to Groper's Grove. Wildflowers—purple, orange, and yellow—was scattered in the clearing between the road and lane, and I waded through them. The lane had been gated years ago and was all growed over. A rusty chain secured the gate, and a "No Trespassing" sign with faded letters hung on the end post. I put my finger to one of the bullet holes in the sign. Prob'ly a .45, I thought. The edges of the holes was rusted.

The chain clanged against the gate as I climbed it and swung my leg over the top rail. I headed down the lane. Brambles, briars, and young trees covered the grove now, and the trunk of an old oak rotted on the ground—a mound of dirt at its base, the shattered canopy long gone. The standing oaks looked the same, but I knowed they had growed bigger.

As I walked through the field, my mind flooded with images of Abigail, Amy, Greg, and rednecks drinking around bonfires and howling at the moon. Them days had been good to me—the best of my life.

Back near the gate, I picked a fistful of flowers. I laid them in the truck and felt under the seat. My hand lighted on the flask, and I hesitated, then reached further and found the spool of string I used for making my work plumb. I unwound some string and sawed through it with my teeth, then tied a knot around the stems. I shoved the spool beneath the seat and heard gravel crunch as I pulled off.

At home, I stepped in the side door.

"Abigail. Abigail!"

She come in the kitchen. "I'm right here. You don't have to ye—"

"Happy anniversary." I held out the flowers.

She lit up, taking them. "They're beautiful!"

Abigail smelt the flowers, set them on the counter, and searched the cabinets. She filled the vase with water and centered it on the table. Finding scissors, she cut the string and trimmed the stems, then slid them down the vase's neck and arranged the flowers, mixing colors. Them daisies stood out.

I scooted a chair from the table, taking a load off. Abigail walked by, and I snagged her waist and spun her to my lap—the way I done when we dated.

"You're frisky today," she said.

"Ain't I always?"

Her hands was on her thighs, and she gripped the scissors, blades closed. I prised them from her and set them on the table.

"What say me and you turn in early?"

She tried to get up, but I pulled her to my lap again, placing one hand on the small of her back, the other on her knee. She used to hang her arm around me, but now her fingers latched on her legs, and when I eased my hand up her thigh, she flexed.

"What the hell?"

"I'm not in the mood right now."

"Right now?" I let her stand. "You ain't never in the mood! How long's it been, huh? Hell, I figured at some point you'd thaw."

She turned from me, and I took her wrist. "It's our anniversary." When she twisted her arm free, blood rushed to my face, making it tingle. I sprung up and snatched her elbow.

"Let go!" she said, swatting me away.

My stomach felt on fire, and my hands started shaking. I didn't regret nothing I had ever done in Jim Sumner's barn—although I sometimes felt bad when I seen Abigail and thought about that girl. But suddenly, Abigail had snuffed out what little guilt I had, and I wanted to tell her the consequences of her never being in the mood.

Them memories from the barn could usually tide me over, but I knowed thinking about that girl wouldn't be enough tonight, and when Abigail blocked me twiced more, I shot my hand out.

"No!" Her voice was almost a growl.

She tried to push from me, but I clutched a wad of hair in my fist. When she started slapping the table, I realized she was groping for the scissors. I yanked her to her knees. She wrapped her fingers around my forearm, digging her claws deep in my skin. I held firm. She opened her mouth as if to scream, but all that come out was a squeak. Her lower lip quivered.

"I could take it," I said, and leaned down, staring her in the eye. With my other hand, I grabbed the front of her shirt and jerked, ripping off the top two buttons. They skittered across the wood floor. Her bra and her cleavage and her smooth flesh was exposed, and I forced my hand inside the cup and squeezed her tit, hard. "I could motherfuckin' take it!"

I let go and stood over her. She was on her elbows and knees with both hands holding her head, her tit hanging out. I took a step back, pulling loose strands of hair from my fingers. "Ain't seen you in that position in years."

I walked out, leaving the door wide open.

Book III

Jesse VII

The Scent

Pop washed up past Shiloh Bridge. The cops in Lincoln County claimed he had shot himself and his body had been beaten by logs and rocks while flowing downstream, but that had sounded fishy to me, and I wondered if they was in cahoots with whoever had throwed Pop in the river.

Nadine had told me about Pop. I had been working late with Conley when she had found us at the sawmill. They had stayed with me at the trailer while I packed for the road, then promised to come to Pop's service. In my numbness on the drive home, my thoughts was as scattered as them flies when I had stepped up to the dead lizard. The miles had flown by. At some point, I realized I had forgot to thank Conley for giving me time off.

During the six years I had been in Cullman, Mamma and Pop's marriage had growed worse. I didn't know no details—only how Pop would disappear for days. So when he wasn't home for a few nights, Mamma hadn't thought nothing of it—until Sheriff Castleberry had parked in the drive one morning.

I had asked Mamma why Pop would be in Tennessee, but she didn't have no clue. She said it might've had something to do with gambling—which was news to me—but we both knew Lincoln County was a long way to go when folks closer to home was willing to take his cash.

So I started thinking he was shot somewhere else and the killer took his body to Elk River. If that was the case, I doubted we would learn where he was murdered or why—although the why probably included not enough money or too much whiskey.

The rains hadn't helped none neither. The clouds had busted about the time Pop went missing, and floods made rivers swuft and muddy for days, so his body could've drifted miles before it surfaced.

It wasn't until they found Pop's truck near Sewanee—nearly a hundred miles away—that Lincoln County cops considered something other than suicide. Then they got on a highway robbery kick, saying someone killed him in a holdup and hid his truck. But they didn't have no leads, and they sure wasn't sniffing around to pick up the scent.

When I thought about Pop's death, sometimes I figured he got what he deserved, but other times I wondered if somebody had wronged him. Whatever had happened, the fact I would never see him again hadn't sunk in, and it seemed like he was just on a hunting trip. I wondered if death with close blood always seemed unreal or if it was the shock of the unexpected—or maybe it was because I felt like me and Pop had unsettled business.

I had wished Pop dead plenty, but as I had looked in the closet at his clothes and, later, at his work gloves on the porch railing where he had last laid them, I realized I hadn't wanted him to die—I had wanted him to change.

Somehow his death had reminded me of when he had melted in the shadows after Mamma had pulled the trigger that night we tussled. I remembered walking down the hall and hearing Mamma sob in her bedroom through the closed door. I remembered standing on the porch—shotgun in hand but unable to go further—watching the smooth motion of the axe rising and falling in the glow of the light bulb. And I remembered dozing on the sofa with the gun across my lap, the ring of metal echoing over the yard. It had sounded far away.

Now, as I sat in the swing, looking past Pop's stained gloves still laying on the rail, I stared at the shed. Firewood was stacked in rows beneath the slanted tin roof, and the axe blade was dug in the edge of the chopping block, the handle pointing toward nothing. I wondered where Pop was.

"Ready to go?"

I stood. "Yes ma'am." The swing tapped against my leg.

"You look like a hundred bucks." Mamma straightened my tie. "We're late."

"We're just not quite as early."

When Pop's body had been found, Sheriff Castleberry had identified him. He had told Mamma he didn't want her seeing Pop swolled up and bruised. And yesterday, when the undertaker had called, he recommended the family not view

Pop, based on the damage to Pop's head—damage caused by the bullet's exit. "I did my best," he had said, "but the face doesn't resemble your father." Mamma wasn't sure at first, but I had finally convinced her none of us should see Pop in that condition. "If we see him like that," I had told her, "we won't remember him no other way." It had been the only time I had protected her from Pop.

Me and Mamma picked up Granny, then met Nana Beulah and Papa Jacob at the funeral home. Everyone lingered near Pop's closed coffin, making small talk in quiet voices, but we flocked to Aunt Jackie and Uncle Dewayne when they come in. Mamma had never seen Aunt Jackie pregnant, so she made a fuss, but she was disappointed they had left their two-year-old with a babysitter. I noticed Granny had stayed in her chair. I doubted she knew what was happening since she never showed no emotion, but then she bowed her head and sniffled as Papa Jacob led us in prayer. After the "Amen", the undertaker said he would open the parlor doors soon, so guests could pay their respects.

Pop's visitation was more crowded than I had expected. Friends and church members come to support Mamma, but I suspected some people just wanted to gossip. Whenever I passed clusters of folks, whispers stopped, and eyes darted at me. It made me think of when everybody at the sawmill had hovered around the bloodstained dirt, speculating on why Earle had shot Billy Tucker.

So, for the most part, I stood beside Mamma at Pop's casket. We had flowers and a framed picture of him on the lid. Pop had been about twenty in the photograph—leaning against the bed of his truck, arms crossed. Mamma had said she liked the picture because Pop looked handsome and it reminded her of better days.

"We had some good times too, didn't we?" she had said as we sorted through photos, spreading them on the kitchen table. Them pictures made our lives look normal.

"Yes," I had said—not lying but not feeling truthful neither—"we had good times too." I had seen a photograph from Christmas morning where me and Pop was playing with plastic army men. Pop was sprawled on the carpet, propped on his elbow. Another one showed us sitting outside with toy construction trucks. The bulldozer and grader was smoothing a road in the dirt, and I remembered how dust had stung my eyes as the dump truck had emptied its bucket.

But the good times wasn't as good as they could've been because I never knew when Pop's switch would flip. He reminded me of the dog we had when I was little. I hadn't thought twice about petting her until she snapped at me. Mamma had said it was because she was almost blind and I had surprised her while she had been eating—but I had never petted her again without being ready to jerk my hand away.

Mamma had choked up while we had rifled through the photos. Then she had gathered herself and forced a smile. When she had set the picture on the table, I had seen Pop with his arm around me. I was wearing my jersey and shoulder pads and holding my helmet. We was standing in our yard before a game. It was the first year I had played football.

"I'm sorry, Jesse," a voice said.

I blinked, and them images disappeared. Mr. McCullough stood in front of me. I thanked him and shook his hand, which was all I done with most people in line. But when Mr. Smith stepped up, I mentioned his hay fields and how much I appreciated him hiring me each summer. He said I was the best worker he ever had. He gripped my hand as we spoke, and I wondered if I would be that strong when I turned old. With Tammy Weldon, I felt a lump in my throat. She said Mamma kept her updated on me. I asked about her son and Katheryn, and I recalled the time Katheryn had sat on the floor beside me with her legs curled beneath her, playing with a doll. Tammy said David built a house in town and had two children, and then she pointed across the room. A pretty girl was sitting on the couch with her hands in her lap. I had noticed her earlier, but I hadn't realized it was Katheryn. Tammy said I should go speak with her. When Tammy hugged me, I seen Brenda Allen talking with another woman in line. Brenda had put on weight, and she was wiping away tears with a tissue. I slipped off and walked toward the couch.

Suddenly, someone grabbed my arm. "Hey, boy." The voice reminded me of Pop, and for a second, my mind went dark, and I whipped my head around, expecting to see Pop. When everything come into focus, I didn't recognize the man. His intense stare and the whites of his eyes made him look crazy. He leaned close and, in a low voice, said, "You gonna get the bastards what killed your Pop?".

I tried to pull free, but it was like a vice had clamped my bicep. He was as strong as Pop.

"If you want help," he said, "let me know." An old lady beside him watched me, her face blank. Then the man leaned in again and whispered, "We'll make them sons of bitches pay".

He let go, and I seen part of a tattoo below his shirt sleeve. As I walked away, I looked over my shoulder. He still stared at me with them crazy eyes. I stepped between a few folks toward Katheryn. She stood.

"Sorry about your father."

"Thanks," I said. She smelled like flowers.

She looked down, and I glanced at the man. His back was to me. He rocked on his boot heels, arms crossed. Just past him, Brenda smushed Mamma against her.

I turned to Katheryn. "I didn't know who you was. You're taller." She was different in lots of ways.

"You look the same."

I slid my hands in my pockets. "Your mom said you graduated."

She nodded. I glanced at the man in line again.

"I remember the day you left. Your mother came to see us."

We searched for something to say.

"Do you like Cullman?"

"It's alright, I reckon."

"I wish I could leave town—at least for a while."

"Where would you go?"

She shrugged. "Anywhere."

"Ever been to Cullman?"

She shook her head. "Is it big?"

"Bigger'n here."

Katheryn smiled and touched her necklace. "That ain't saying much."

Tammy joined us. "Are you ready?" she said to Katheryn. Then she turned toward me. "Come have dinner with us one evening."

Katheryn's eyes growed wide.

Tammy hugged me. "Take care of your mother."

"Yes ma'am."

She stepped back, raising her eyebrows and pointing at me. "I'm serious about dinner."

"Yes ma'am."

"Goodbye, Jesse Hartline."

I felt a tingle in my stomach, and I wanted Katheryn to say the rest, but they walked off. She didn't look back.

A finger pecked my shoulder. I turned and seen Tommy Williams. He had been our varsity quarterback and had married his high school sweetheart. He pumped my hand like we was best buddies. We chatted about several players from our football team, then he mentioned how his dad had enjoyed standing along the fence with Pop during games. Me and Tommy probably talked more in the funeral home than we had in school.

As he was leaving, I remembered his wife's name. "Tell Connie I said hello."

"A'ight," he said. "If she'll ever speak to me again." If I hadn't recognized Tommy any other way, I would've knowed him by his laugh—all buck teeth and quick breaths from his nose. Me and other teammates had made fun of it, but he had never cared.

I hadn't seen Murry since working at the filling station, so I figured I should thank him for coming. He stood in a circle of men, including the sheriff in uniform. Mr. Sumner was among them, hat in hand, but I didn't know the others. One was on crutches, facing away from me, and when he glanced to the side, I could tell he was younger. I didn't see Mrs. Sumner.

I recalled standing on the Sumner porch as rain had blowed on me—and how I had been splitting firewood for them when I decided to leave home. It seemed ages ago.

As I headed toward the group of men, Billy Tucker stepped in front of me. He was with Linda. Rumor had it him and Earle had patched things up, but today I had noticed they stayed on opposite sides of the parlor. We spoke for a minute, then Billy said Fred wanted to see me, so I followed him through the crowd.

Fred was beside a man with a beer gut, white hair, and forearms the size of my calves. When Fred seen me, he started shaking his head. "I'm plum tore up about Donny. He was a fine man—and the best mechanic they was." He smacked his lips. "We'll shore miss him at the garage."

"You was Pop's favorite boss." Pop had never said one way or the other, but Fred had always been good to me, and it seemed like a nice thing to say. "Would you mind gatherin' his tools? I'll swing by the shop this week."

"I'll do it first thang Mondee mornin'." He seen me eyeing the man with white hair. Fred pointed his thumb at him. "This here's Cobble."

Cobble's grip was firm. "You have no idea how sorry I was to hear about your daddy."

I thanked him. "How'd you know Pop?"

Somebody squeezed the back of my neck, and I looked sideways. I spun and hugged Conley and Nadine. I had felt beat down until then. My eyes burned. "Thought y'all wasn't gonna make it." We stepped off to the side. Conley asked about Pop, and I told him I hadn't heard nothing new since leaving Cullman a few days ago.

"You may never learn the truth," he said. "Sometimes, even small towns keep secrets."

I walked them to the line to speak with Mamma, then strode toward Murry. Only Mr. Sumner and the sheriff stood with him now.

Mr. Sumner fiddled with his hat when he spoke. "I hate what happened to your father."

Murry nodded. "I learnt a lot from your old man. He knowed ever'thing about motors—and he kept us in stitches."

I remembered Pop making wisecracks at the garage, but I was usually the only person not laughing. Murry had clapped me on the back once after Pop told a dirty joke: "Get it?". Pop had spit tobacco juice, then said, "One day, Murry, he'll understand". They both had laughed.

Someone said something, and I snapped out of it. Sheriff Castleberry had his hand stretched toward me. "Take care," he said, probably for the second time. We shook. "If you or your mother need anything, just holler."

Mr. Sumner gave a nod and put on his hat as he left with the sheriff.

"Your Mamma's a firecracker," Murry said, "but this'll dampen her spirit." He lowered his eyes and toed at the carpet.

"Excuse me," a man said, stepping from the wall. "You're Donny's boy, ain't chee?" Deep creases lined his brow. The lady with him had grey hair piled in a thick bun on top of her head, reminding me of a hornet's nest.

"You don't know us," he said, "but this is my wife, Wilma." She smiled, her lips tight. "And I'm Richard— although I used to go by Ricky."

It took a moment to register. I knew him—but only by name.

"Your kinfolk won't look my way," he said. "Can't says I blame them." He wrung his hands, and his dark eyes went bloodshot. "They won't never believe it, but I'm a differ'nt person now. I found the Lord, and I'm a differ'nt person." He reached in his pocket. "I'm sorry about Donny.

I truly am. Please tell them." As we shook hands, he said, "He raised you right". Wilma followed him out the door.

He had pressed something in my palm. I looked down and opened my hand. It was a crisp dollar bill, folded twice. What the heck, I thought.

I walked over and plopped on the couch. I rested my eyes a minute, then noticed Mamma speaking to a man in a suit. He leaned forward, and I couldn't tell if he whispered in her ear or kissed her cheek, but something flashed across her face. As the man turned, I seen it was Mr. Smith's son. He had hauled hay with us once, but all he done was run the tractor while everybody else worked.

After stepping from Mamma, Jefferey stooped in front of Granny's chair and spoke to her. Granny couldn't stay on her feet for long, so she would stand with Mamma for a while, then sit for a spell. I wondered if she remembered driving to Jefferey's house.

Conley and Nadine was next in line, and Mamma looked happy to see them. Nadine held Mamma's hand as they talked. Only a couple of folks stood behind Conley, and I figured Mamma was wore out and ready to visit with Aunt Jackie and Uncle Dewayne. They had loaded their car with food people had brung and took it to our house with Nana Beulah and Papa Jacob.

For the past hour, the man who had grabbed my arm had kept crossing my mind. I didn't know what he expected me to do or why he was willing to help. Then chills run through me. I jumped up and scanned the room. He was gone.

I settled back on the couch. How did he know to say "them", I thought. I closed my eyes again and smelled perfume. Or maybe it was the flowers on the end table. Either way, Katheryn come to mind. I recalled her shy smile and how she had shifted from one foot to the other as we had talked. Then I thought about the look she gave her mother, and I wondered whether or not Katheryn wanted me to come to dinner.

Abigail VII

Out of the Dust

My eyes snapped open. I was laying on the couch, not sure what had startled me awake. Then somebody banged on the door, rattling the glass. I had accidentally locked Donny out, and he was trying—my throat knotted.

I remembered seeing the sheriff's car pull in the drive, crumpling on the porch steps, and asking Greg if he was certain Donny was dead. Greg said he had identified the body himself. Later, I realized I hadn't been thinking straight and should have asked more questions, especially after Greg said they suspected suicide.

When Greg had asked if I knew why Donny would kill himself, I recalled the rumor someone from the diner had spread, and I wondered if Donny had heard those lies. But even if Donny had believed them, he wouldn't take his own life over it. He would have more likely killed Jefferey—or me. My bet was Donny had gotten into trouble gambling. But I met Greg's eyes and said, "Nothing comes to mind".

"Anyone have a grudge against him?"

I thought of Jesse and my parents, what Conley had said about Donny, and what Gladdis had almost said before catching herself when she had found me on the side of the road. Then I considered how Donny had stopped doing odd jobs for Jim when they had an argument concerning pay. And I remembered Jefferey making the comment about Donny being out of the picture. Those people had flashed through my mind in a blink, but none of them were murderers.

"I'm sure that list is long." I glanced at Greg's nose. "And includes you."

Greg pursed his lips, then shook his head. "I let that slide a long time ago."

After Greg had driven away, I felt lightheaded when I stood. I wondered why he would ask about grudges if he thought Donny committed suicide. Greg's nose had reminded me of Donny jumping him at the poolhall, and how, after their fight, Amy had broken up with Greg and left for college. He had as much reason to hold a grudge against Donny as anyone. *Almost* anyone—but Greg and I weren't murderers either.

Then it struck me how I had cocked the pistol when Donny had stepped toward me. If he could push his wife to the brink . . .

Greg was wrong, I thought. It wasn't suicide.

I leaned against the pillar at the top of the stairs, staring toward the empty shed and thinking about Donny working out his frustrations on the chopping block. Then I looked down and noticed each concrete step was worn smooth in the middle, and I saw dried mud from Greg's boot on the bottom step. I remembered scolding Donny for tracking mud in the house, how I had always been the one who swept, and how I had never looked at a broom the same after being hit with the broken handle. I recalled sitting on the swing with Donny, his arm around me or his hand running up and down my thigh. Then I saw his work gloves—one on top of the other—resting on the railing. The hands that had filled them had been coarse and gentle and loving and hurtful. Beside the gloves stood the last empty beer bottle I would ever clean from the porch. I wept.

When my head cleared, I thought about the phone calls I needed to make: to Jesse, my parents, Granny. I walked in the house and picked up the receiver, then hung it back on the hook and collapsed on the couch. My eyelids grew heavy as I pieced together my conversation with Greg. I thought of his bent nose again, and how Amy had escaped everything by leaving town, and I wondered if—under different circumstances—I would have done the same. Jackie had said she had learned from my mistake, and she and Dewayne had gone off to college, earned degrees, and built their life elsewhere. I wouldn't trade Jesse for a degree or anything the world offered, so I had told her Jesse wasn't a mistake—he was my prize.

Now, fully awake, I realized I had fallen asleep and been dreaming about Donny when something had startled me. Then I heard frantic knocks. I stood and peeped around the corner. Father had his hands cupped to the glass, peering through the window.

"Greg called us," Mother said, as I opened the door. She hugged me. "We were worried sick when you didn't answer."

I remembered hearing the phone ring but thinking it was part of my dream.

The shock of losing my husband, the confusion from the uncertainty of how he died, and the realization he would never hurt me again swirled in my mind, and I melted in Father's embrace. I felt like a little girl again as he held me tight. When I stepped from him, his eyes were red, and it dawned on me how the only other time I had seen him cry was when he had first cradled Jesse in his arms.

In the house, I told them Greg thought Donny had shot himself. Then they spouted out questions I couldn't answer—perhaps no one could answer—with so many missing pieces to the puzzle.

"Well, I'm not surprised," Mother said. "Donny rubbed people the wrong way."

"Don't speak ill of the dead, Beulah."

"I'm sorry, dear," she said to me. She adjusted her bracelets. "But you know it's true."

Father wagged his head. Then he asked if Granny knew, and we decided to tell her in person. He drove, and on the way to Granny's, I stared out the window.

Highs and lows with Donny swam in my head—but the lows were more buoyant. I recalled our anniversary several years ago, which had been a turning point. After that day, I couldn't look at Donny for a while, and without Jesse, we had nothing to discuss. Jesse had been my focus for eighteen years, and when he left, it seemed as though half the town had moved away.

I was lonely but not alone, and the house was empty of joy and full of resentment. I slept in Jesse's room, and

Donny and I avoided one another and found chores to keep us busy. When Donny was home, he stayed outside most of the time. If it rained, he went to the shed or watched television. Some evenings he would disappear for hours. Over the last month, it had turned into days. But, to his credit, he continued working at Fred's. I didn't know if he slept in his truck, at the garage, or somewhere else, but I no longer cared.

I still tended laundry and cooked, and we occasionally ate together. After supper, I would gaze out the window over the sink and feel my way around the dishes. I usually thought about Jesse playing in the yard with his favorite toys through the years. He would set up his action figures and use dirt clods for bombs, make racecourses for his toy cars, and punt the football, walking to where it had landed and kicking it the other direction. Sometimes I thought of Jesse and Evan practicing football plays, how quiet Jesse had been when Evan had run away, and how I had written Evan's mother trying to console her but had never felt comfortable mailing the letter.

Then one evening, out of the blue, Donny thanked me for dinner, which marked the beginning of our being cordial to each other. A few nights later, he joked about how I had missed him when I had shot over his head, and he said we should shoot together like the old days, so I could improve my marksmanship.

I didn't know if he hoped to relieve tension or wanted me in the bedroom, but I guessed, in his own way, he was saying he was sorry. Still, he should have known it was too little, too late. I had grown used to our routine, and for a long time, the only thing I had missed concerning Donny and me was the possibility of what we could have been.

If he had made any effort on our relationship years ago, we may not have drifted so far apart, but I eventually wore out from trying for both of us. I could still hear his response when I told him relationships required a lot of work. "I work at work," he had said. "Only so much work a man can do." But he would always be rebuilding engines, cleaning the yard, or splitting firewood, so he worked at home plenty, and it hurt my feelings to know I wasn't worth the effort. So, toward the end, no amount of kindness could fill the gap between us, and his last-ditch attempts to make peace had saddened me.

To escape the house, I picked up shifts at the diner. When I had been a waitress in high school, dealing with customers had been stressful. But after years of raising a child and living with Donny, serving customers and managing orders were a breeze.

But extra hours meant more interaction with Jefferey, and now, sitting in the back seat on the way to Granny's, I remembered when Jefferey had given me a ride to her house and how we had talked in his driveway afterwards, and my last conversation with him at the diner came to mind.

"When should we drop off Mrs. Hartline's car again?" he had said.

It had been lunchtime, and customers had been in booths on both sides of him. I had noticed a slight movement from the corner of my eye. Jim Sumner sat in the next booth, and he had cocked his ear toward us. I made sure Jefferey saw my eyes flash at Jim. "What did you think about my Sunday school lesson?"

Jefferey glanced over his shoulder and raised his voice, ignoring my worry. "I liked how you related our daily trials and tribulations to the Bible. What was it—sorrow and whispering dust?"

"Thy speech shall whisper out of the dust."

Jim swung one leg from the booth, twisting toward me. "Pardon my intrusion. Could you oblige me by reciting the rest?"

I quoted the Scripture.

"Where can I find that verse? I want to share it with the spouse."

I jotted the book and chapter on a ticket, ripped it from my pad, and handed it to Jim. "More coffee?"

"No thank you, sweetie. I have an engagement." He donned his hat, pinched the brim, and left.

In the booth on the other side of Jefferey, four teenagers were laughing and carrying on.

"See?" I said in a low voice. "People listen."

"Let them listen."

"You never know how someone will interpret what you say—or how they might repeat it. That's how rumors start."

"Afraid he'll tell Gladdis we discussed your mother-in-law's car?"

I considered spilling coffee in Jefferey's lap, but it would have caused a scene.

"Besides," he said, "we're not fooling around. At least, not yet."

"Hush!" I scanned the room. Nobody was watching, but I felt like everyone had heard. I slid his check on the table. "Don't you have court?"

"Yes ma'am. But first, I need to give Mrs. Hartline a ride."

I turned and walked away, fighting a smile.

Then today—four days later—Greg had pulled into my drive, and now I felt guilt for having flirted with Jefferey so near Donny's death, and I hoped Jim had not suspected anything was going on between us.

"Should we all go in?" Father said.

I realized we were at Granny's. I nodded.

Granny didn't seem surprised by our visit and invited us inside. When I told her Donny had passed away, her face remained blank.

"My little Donny?" she finally said.

I hugged her. "I'm so sorry." Tears rolled down my cheeks.

When I stepped back, she looked at each of us, then said to no one in particular, "How old was he?".

My heart broke for her. "He was forty-four, Granny."

She nodded slowly. "That's what I thought."

I looked at Father.

"Do you want us to stay with you?" he said.

"I'm not a child. I can care for myself."

I patted her arm. "He means do you want company?"

She leveled her eyes at me. "I know what he meant, deary."

As we were leaving, Granny watched from the side door, and I wondered if she would ask this time. Then, when I was halfway across the carport, she called my name. I turned, the reply on the tip of my tongue.

"Where's my car?"

"We borrowed it."

"I need to get groceries."

Donny and I had been taking her to the store or delivering her groceries ever since Jesse had moved to Cullman. "I'll bring it back shortly."

She thought for a second. "That'll be fine." She closed the door, and I heard the lock bolt.

I convinced Mother and Father I was alright to remain home by myself, then dialed Jesse's number. After twenty rings, I hung up and tried Nadine. She said Jesse and Conley had stayed late at the sawmill, trying to catch up from when Conley had missed a couple of days of work. I told her about Donny, and she insisted on driving to the mill to find them if they didn't answer the office phone. When Nadine returned my call, she said Jesse had packed and was already on the road.

I waited for him on the couch, listening to the ring of silence.

Everything was a whirlwind from when Jesse arrived until after Donny's funeral. I remembered crying as I had hugged Jesse, sifting through family photos, and my excitement at seeing Jackie pregnant. I also recalled the crowded funeral parlor and not recognizing everyone and, later, wondering if the people I hadn't seen in years had crawled out of the woodwork from sympathy or suspected scandal.

I only remembered a few conversations from visitation: Tammy saying the Sunday school class would provide supper this week, being squashed against Brenda and almost smiling when I realized why Jesse had slipped off, and nearly falling into Conley's strong arms when he and Nadine had spoken to me. But my clearest memory was Jefferey. I had seen him in line and avoided eye contact, and as he had stood in front of me, I had wished he had not come. He had shaken my hand and stepped close, his breath warm on my ear. "You're a free woman," he had whispered. I had imagined Jefferey's joy when he had learned Donny died, and I didn't want anyone thinking I felt the same. Conley and Nadine had waited behind Jefferey, and I hoped they hadn't overheard.

Now, sitting on my living-room couch, I was thankful to them and the whole family for supporting me when we had buried Donny today. Jackie was nestled beside me, and I kept placing my hand on her stomach, feeling tiny kicks. Granny called it "slinging shoes". Nadine brought Conley a plate of food and asked if anybody else wanted anything. Mother and Father sat on the loveseat while Jesse talked to Dewayne and thumbed through the visitation sign-in book.

"I never seen Gladdis Sumner."

"She wasn't there," I said. Jesse had jogged my memory, and Jim's apology came to mind. "Jim said she was under the weather."

"Says here, 'Jim and Gladdis Sumner'."

"That's cheating," Nadine said. "But I've signed for Conley when he couldn't be somewhere."

Without looking up, Jesse said, "Who is James Tinker?".

"He built Granny's house when she moved out and sold us this one," I said. "Donny helped him on weekends. Granny, do you remember Mr. Tinker?"

"Who?"

"James Tinker."

"Oh, yes," she said. "Nice young man."

I eyed her.

"Taught Donny carpentry—although Donny said he was more suited for a mechanic."

I smiled. "That's right. Except Mr. Tinker must be seventy by now."

"He was tall for a carpenter," Granny said.

I smiled again.

"That reminds me," Conley said. "Who was the lanky guy in front of us at the funeral home?"

I felt my face flush. I told him Jefferey's name, feeling Mother's stare.

"When he learned we were cousins, he sang your praises. Said you were the best waitress in town."

Mother cleared her throat. "Well, he happens to be the best lawyer in town."

Father put his hand on her leg and squeezed.

"That explains it," Conley said.

I wanted to ask what he meant. Instead, I asked Jackie if she snacked as much as I did when I was pregnant.

"I eat ice cream every day!"

"What about Lester Slatton?"

Dewayne looked at Jesse. "Lester Slatton? Haven't thought of him in years."

"Who is he?"

"He dropped out of school a year or two before graduation. Tried to sell me dope once." Dewayne turned toward me. "Did Donny know Lester?"

I shrugged. "Beats me. Donny hardly mentioned anybody."

"What does he look like?"

"Couldn't tell you now," Dewayne said, "but he used to be thin as a rail with thick red hair."

Jesse turned the page.

"Well," Dewayne said, standing and stretching, "it's about that time." He helped Jackie to her feet. They were sleeping at our parents' house again and leaving early in the morning.

I asked Granny to stay with Jesse and me, but she said she had a busy day tomorrow, so Father offered her a ride. I was afraid she would see her car and say she could drive herself, but she walked past it without a second look.

Jackie and I had a long goodbye, and I promised to visit her newborn when they returned from the hospital.

"We should probably get rolling too," Conley said.

"You must be worn out," Nadine said to me.

Conley told Jesse to take as much time as he needed, then he hugged me and said, "We're one call away". As they drove off, I watched their taillights until they rounded the curve, wondering what Conley really thought about Donny's death.

Jesse and I stayed on the porch. The front door was open, so I pushed the bottom of the screen door with my foot, sealing out bugs, then sat on the swing with Jesse. The chains creaked as we swung.

Night fell.

"When are you eating dinner at Tammy's? She's trying to set you up with Katheryn—even though I reminded her you don't live here."

"Hm? Oh. Tuesday, but I'm not sure I'm going."

"I told her Katheryn was too young for you anyway." He didn't react. "Still, she's a beautiful girl." He nodded slightly. I couldn't tell if he was not interested, pretending not to be interested, or distracted.

Moths fluttered around the porch light, and the screen wire twanged when insects flew into it. I stared beyond the edge of the light. Flashes floated across the yard as the last of the fireflies drifted through the darkness. With autumn around the corner, the crickets, cicadas, katydids, and treefrogs were singing their final songs for the season, and the nights ahead would be silent.

A gentle breeze held off the mugginess, and the weather made me think of the pride I had felt watching Jesse's games on Fridays.

"Do you miss playing football this time of year?"

Jesse remained quiet for a minute. Then, from nowhere, he said, "Did you talk to the man with crazy eyes?", and I knew he meant Marlon.

Donny VII

Dog Days

"You sure it's okay? I hate to leave you in a lurch on the weekend."

"I'll manage," Mr. Buffington had said. He had slipped me a twenty from the register. "Take her someplace nice."

I had headed for the door.

"Donny," Mr. Buffington had said, and he had that familiar tone. I had turned and paused, holding the handle. He had stared at me over his glasses. "Treat her like a lady."

I had winked, then walked out.

Halfway to the truck, I had heard Mr. Buffington say, "Let me be more specific". I had stopped and seen him propping open the door with his arm. "Keep your pecker in your pants."

"Yes sir," I had said. The folks in the parking lot had laughed.

The next day I had learnt Mr. Buffington had been shot and killt while I had been on my date with Abigail. He had discharged one of the two barrels from his shotgun and blowed a hole in the ceiling—telling me the other man had fired first.

Now, neighborhood of twenty-five years later, I sat on the hood of my truck, staring at the old silo. The other man, I thought. What I wouldn't give for a name. Mr. Buffington's death weighed heavy on my mind tonight, and I wondered if the killer was still out there somewhere or if he had met a faster draw.

I bit off a plug of tobacco and laid the pouch beside my pistol. The barrel looked like blue steel under Fred's nightlight.

This evening, me and Fred had replaced the alternator on his wife's car, and after he left, I had putzed around the shop, then come outside. The full moon had climbed above the mountain, and the field glowed. I could even make out the dark sapling on the silo.

Every so often, a vehicle would cruise down the highway, and I'd ease my hand to my side until it passed. But when one slowed to a stop, I wrapped my fingers around the gun's grip. I couldn't see nothing through the headlights, but the rumble of the engine sounded familiar.

"Take your hand off that smoke-wagon."

Weren't no way in hell he could've seen that gun, but I let go, slid from the hood, and walked to the car. It was pitch black inside, then a flame showed the shadowy outline of Cobble's face when he lit a cigarette. Someone rode shotgun. I heard metal snap shut, and the interior went black again—all but a speck of orange. Smoke floated from the open window.

"I need the money."

I realized Cobble hadn't just happened by. I spat to the side. "I'll finish your kitchen this week."

"The hell with the kitchen. I want the money."

"You know I'm good for it."

"Always have been—over time." He held his hand out the window, two fingers raised. "You got two days."

"Why the rush all of a sudden?" But my gut told me the answer.

"Two days." When he flipped the cigarette butt, the cherry splashed at my feet, then went out. "And Donny," he said, his white hair almost glowing as he leaned from the window, "watch yourself." He pulled off, slow. His taillights was dull. Fred's nightlight flickered and hummed.

So, I thought, Cobble somehow caught wind I was being followed, and he suspected my days was numbered.

Over the last few weeks, I had noticed a car tailing me. It would lay back and match my speed and sometimes turn where I turned. At night, the headlights would go out, and it would disappear. Then one afternoon at the shop, I had jumped in the truck and headed toward a car parked in the distance. I had saw two men as the car had whipped around and sped away. Another night, I had been working in the shed and heard a vehicle creeping along. I had walked up the road with my pistol. The engine had been quiet, and the vehicle had drove off before I reached it. On the way back to the shed, I had saw a beer bottle standing upright in the middle of the road. I hadn't knowed if somebody lurked in the shadows or if I had missed it in the dark. I had kicked the bottle toward the ditch and heard the hollow sound of it skidding across the road.

When I had gone inside, I had paced the floor and looked out the window whenever a vehicle went by. "What's gotten into you? You're driving me crazy," Abigail had said. I had told her Murry had said thieves was in the area.

At first, I had supposed whoever was dogging me had just been trying to rattle my cage. But when I learnt they was watching the house, I knowed that river run deeper. So—on the off-chance bullets started flying—I had decided to stay at the garage, steering them clear of Abigail.

After Cobble's taillights faded, I climbed on the hood again. I wondered when them boys would grow a backbone and face me like men. Then I recalled what Cobble had said, and I reckoned he had bartered part of my debt, buying time to collect his money. Or maybe they was his dogs waiting for the signal to pounce. I spat. No, I thought, Cobble handled his own affairs.

I stared across the field in the moonlight, unable to figure out who them boys was and what they wanted. But I knowed what Cobble wanted, and I considered what he might do if I couldn't hold him at bay with a couple hundred bucks. According to rumors, Cobble had persuaded people with more than baseball bats and busted ribs. Still, we had growed to be buddies over the years, so he wouldn't do them things to me. Them lowlifes he roughed up was the caliber of folks who would do anything if they was desperate for cash— even kill. Then a thought struck me: The man who had murdered Mr. Buffington might've owed Cobble. If Cobble remembered anyone who had squared up with him around that time, then me and Marlon would finally have a name— decades after the trail had growed cold.

*

The day after Mr. Buffington was shot, I had looked through the window of the liquor store and seen his blood smeared on the wall behind the register. And even though I tried to keep that image buried, sometimes I would look at Abigail and think about Mr. Buffington blowed against the wall and sliding to the floor while me and her had been spending that twenty bucks he give me. I never admitted to Abigail I had always blamed myself for leaving him alone, so she never knowed a wedge had been drove between us.

When I had told Marlon his daddy died because of me, he had said, "Life goes on, and death goes on". Then he had warned me not to bring up blame again. I never did. I knowed better than to cross Marlon.

After Marlon had let me feel his burr haircut on the day that glass had lodged in my hand, I didn't see him for a long time. But whenever I helped Mr. Buffington, he had talked about his son. When I started working more hours, I heard Marlon stories every day. Then, after my senior year, Marlon had swung by the store more often. He had a tattoo with a sword and lightning bolts on his arm.

Since he hardly never said two words to me, I had figured he must've forgot who I was, so one day when he hung around the counter, I walked up and said, "Remember me?". The whites of his eyes had made his stare intense. "I'm the one that—"

"I know who you are."

Mr. Buffington had watched, glasses on the tip of his nose.

"You're the one that runs my daddy's business."

Mr. Buffington had laughed.

The next time I seen Marlon was at his father's funeral. After speaking to Mrs. Buffington, I had stood in the corner, watching. When I finally got a chance to talk to Marlon, I had asked if we was going to find the bastard that killt his daddy. He had put his hand on my shoulder and squeezed. "Brother," he had said, "you're goddamn right we are."

Me and Marlon drove around the next day, hunting the killer. We spent the better part of two weeks together, asking everybody we seen if they knowed anything about what happened. We went house to house—Jehovah's Witness style—knocking on doors. Some folks didn't answer or wasn't home—others talked to us and told Marlon they was sorry. A few people give names that led to nothing.

We even flagged cars down on the backroads. One truck was already pulled over, and a man come from the woods when we stopped. He spoke first.

"Y'all seen a black bag anywheres?"

I shook my head. His sidekick picked up a CB, mashed the button and mumbled, then laid it on the seat. I glanced at Marlon.

"You seem like the kinda fella who keeps his ear to the ground," I said, and told the man what we was doing.

"Never heerd nothin' about it," he said. "What's it worth to you if I do?"

Marlon leaned over to look him in the eye. "Ever'thing."

We rode on.

We walked through town, stopping folks on the sidewalk, and I told Abigail to eavesdrop at the diner. I had even pegged Ricky as a suspect, and me and Marlon finally tracked down where he lived. As we jostled down the long, dead-end road, I remembered how one morning four or five years ago I had found mom crying in the kitchen. Ricky had took all our cash and valuables and become smoke in the wind. I never knowed if mom was upset about him leaving or the stolt stuff.

At the end of the road, it looked like Ricky had been contemplating getting in the junkyard business. Hubcaps, a couple of rusted lawnmowers, a chrome bumper, and sundry hardware was being swallered by grass and weeds. The porch overflowed with junk. Boxes with dark stains was stacked to the ceiling behind the swing. The nearside chain had either broke or been unhooked, and the swing had a saddle draped over its back. A seatless bicycle propped against a barrel, and a half-coiled water hose hung off the handlebars. Bald tires anchored the tin roof.

Then I noticed a woman sitting on the washing machine on the porch. She had blended in with everything else. We stepped from the truck. When she scooted off the washer, it started rocking. The woman set her cup on the only clear space on the windowsill and stumbled halfway down the sagging stairs. She wore a faded pink robe with a flower on each pocket. Damned if I knowed if she was thirty or sixty.

Marlon told her we was looking for Ricky.

"Ricky's in jail," she said. "Thank Gawd. If you see 'im, tell 'im I said to kiss my ass!"

I reckoned he had done a number on her too. She was barefoot, and her toes wrapped around the lip of the step, next to where a dog had gnawed the corner. Her toenails was painted red.

"I told that sack of shit if he ever come crawlin' back I'd send 'im straight to hell." She pointed her finger and made the sound of a gunshot when she dropped her thumb. She lost her balance but grabbed the wobbly handrail to steady herself. When she straightened up, she brushed her stringy hair from her face.

I almost laughed, but Marlon didn't crack a smile.

"Hey, buster," she said. "Bum a smoke?"

Marlon walked toward her and held up the pack. She took a cigarette, and he lit it for her and backed away. She swayed.

"What you want with Ricky?" The cigarette had bobbed, then dangled from the corner of her mouth.

"Old friend," Marlon said.

"Horseshit. You ain't got no old nothin'."

She looked from Marlon to me and back to Marlon, then slid her hands to her waist, holding her robe open. "You fellers wanna come inside?"

I turned the truck around and headed out. The washboard road jarred us. Marlon smoked. When I eased onto the main road, Marlon said, "She'd 'a' learned you anything you wanted to know—but at a steep price."

That night Mrs. Buffington cooked us dinner. I figured the distraction was good for her even though she'd choke up when we talked about Mr. Buffington. Onc't, when she had excused herself from the table, Marlon had said, "Somewhere out there is a dead man walking". He had pointed at me, dropped his thumb, and made the sound of a distant gunshot.

Over the next month, I hardly had time to piss. Me and Abigail started going steady, Fred hired me, and Mrs. Buffington cooked dinner for me and Marlon a couple nights a week. Marlon searched for his daddy's murderer every day, and I joined him when I could, but we never found no leads.

When Marlon left, I started driving by Mrs. Buffington's house and his trailer after work to keep an eye on things, and I'd sometimes stop to check on Mrs. Buffington. Ever since she had patched my palm, I had been drawed to her. She had brung me and Mr. Buffington lunch at the store now and again, and when she did, I had that same tingle as when she had first touched my hand. I never knowed what made me feel that way, but a bond growed between us, and over time I opened up to her like I never done with nobody.

As the years chugged by, I hated she stayed alone, so I would fix something on her house or do yardwork. Eventually, Thursdays become our evening. She'd usually cook dinner, and then we'd sit in the living room and talk. She mentioned Mr. Buffington a lot. And when she talked about Marlon's visits, she glowed like a kid at Christmas.

I weren't sure why, but I had never told Abigail how close I was to Mrs. Buffington. Maybe I couldn't show that side of me for some reason, or maybe I didn't think she'd understand—or, maybe, I just liked holding secrets. Whatever the case, Mrs. Buffington knowed me inside and out. With Abigail, I was only skin deep.

Now, sitting on that hood, I reminisced about my first meal with Marlon and Mrs. Buffington and how tough I had felt tracking a killer with a Ranger. I had only been eighteen—same age as Jesse when he moved to Cullman six years ago—but I'd wager he had felt growed up too.

I remembered my conversation with Marlon the day before he had disappeared for a spell, and how he had made me promise to take care of his mother if he never come home.

"Why wouldn't you come home?" I had said.

Marlon had turned and lifted his shirt, showing me the scar. "That's where it come out."

"Christ Almighty," I had said, and then promised.

I run my thumb over my palm and thought about that chunk of glass. I recalled the sting and how it had gouged my raw flesh, and I imagined the considerable pain tied to Marlon's scar. Then I thought of the different type of pain he had suffered when our manhunt had kept leading down dead ends. Marlon had been hellbent for revenge, but he had never quenched that bloodthirst.

I hooked my bootheels on the bumper. Of all my summers, I thought, two stood out. The first one, I started dating Abigail, Mr. Buffington was killt, and Abigail got pregnant. Then the other—all them years later—that girl showed up in the barn, and Jesse moved away. Maybe it was the August heat or something in the thick air, but now here we was again—at the tail end of the dog days—and I knowed this summer weren't no slouch.

But even though it felt like the noose was tightening, I mulled over what Cobble had said. I spat toward the fencepost in front of the truck, thinking how I was due for a hot shower and change of clothes, and how my back ached from sleeping on the cot in the shop. I decided to stretch out in my own bed tonight.

The hood popped out when I slid off, and I tossed my gun through the open window. It bounced on the seat—then I seen the book. My knees almost buckled. I leaned against the truck and looked at Fred's nightlight. A bat swooped amongst the swarming bugs, then doubled back. The light hummed and flickered.

Jesse VIII

The Winning Hand

I smelled coffee when I stepped in the house. Mamma sat at the kitchen table, her hands cupped around a mug. She wore her waitress uniform, and it struck me how she was never the one being served. I asked if she wanted anything.

"I'm just resting my feet. I worked part of Gail's shift. You know, I think she's pregnant."

Today was Mamma's first day at the diner since Pop's funeral. She planned to work extra hours for the missed time, but she also hoped to make up for the gambling money she was convinced Pop had lost.

"How was Joe's?"

"Like you'd expect. Lots of people saying they're sorry. Some whispers."

Pop's death had taken a toll on Mamma, and she looked older. I wondered how much longer she could serve full time and how she would survive if she had to quit.

I earned good money in Cullman—enough for both of us—but I could help her in other ways if I lived here. And considering how supper at the Weldon's had gone, I got the idea it was time to move home. But I would hate to leave the sawmill—and Conley and Nadine.

Mamma lifted her cup. "Maybe just a warmup."

She folded her hands in her lap as I poured.

"Cream?"

She nodded.

I reached in the refrigerator, then placed the small carton in front of her.

"Would you like anything else, ma'am?"

"Oh, hush."

As I sat across from her, she pulled sugar packets from her pocket and dropped them in the basket on the table. She emptied a packet in her coffee and added cream.

"Does Joe know you steal from the diner?" I tried to keep a straight face.

"For your information, I had forgotten they were in my pocket."

"That mug looks awful familiar."

"You hush!" I seen a hint of her old smile, then she sighed. "Remember the candy?"

I thought about the time Pop had gone to the store for tobacco. I had tagged along, and coming home, I had started eating a candy bar. Pop had asked how I had bought it. When I didn't answer, his face had turned red. "We ain't thieves," he had said. He had snatched the candy and swung the truck around, then dragged me in the store to apologize and promise never to steal. I had blubbered as Pop had laid the candy bar beside the register and paid the owner. He had left the candy on the counter. At home, Pop had led me to the kitchen by my ear. "Tell your Mamma what you done." I had cried again.

Now, I looked across the table in that same kitchen. "He cured me from stealing."

"He had his moments." She picked up a spoon and stirred. "Did you find him?"

I nodded.

"What did he say?" Her spoon clinked against the inside of the mug.

I wasn't sure what to tell her, so I thought through my conversation with Marlon.

When I had parked at Marlon's trailer, he had shut off the lawnmower and strode toward me. His white t-shirt had damp sweat marks, and the bottom of his tattoo showed beneath the sleeve. He had stared at me with them crazy eyes.

"Knowed you'd come," he said, reaching for his shirt pocket. He slid out the cigarette pack and extended it.

"Don't smoke."

"Neither did your Pop. But he always took one." He grinned, then his eyes went distant.

Marlon's comment from the funeral home had constantly crossed my mind over the past week. Mamma had said Marlon and Pop had hunted together, and she had told me about the Buffingtons selling their liquor store after Marlon's father had died. But she hadn't knowed much else, other than where his mother lived. At first, I had decided against tracking him down, but as I had become more desperate to learn what had happened to Pop, I had told Mamma I wanted to find the man called Marlon.

He pulled a cigarette from the pack with his mouth, then shielded the lighter. Marlon blowed out smoke. "Your daddy thought the world of you."

He must've seen my surprise.

Marlon nodded. "He was proud of you, boy. Always talking about your football games and bragging how strong you was. Said you could whup anybody in high school." He paused. "Tough as nails."

I had doubts about trusting Marlon—until then. I recalled Pop's crow's-feet, and Marlon had similar wrinkles around his eyes. Then I remembered the first time Pop took the belt to me and how I hadn't cried, but my pretending to be tough had only led to harder swats.

"How you wanna handle them bastards what killed your Pop?" He dropped his cigarette and toed it with his boot, then lit another. His boots had grass stains.

"They said Pop shot himself."

He squinted. "Then why'd you come here?"

Marlon was smarter than I had given him credit for, and I was beginning to think he wasn't crazy. "How do you know who done it?"

"The night your Pop disappeared, he checked on my trailer. He hadn't knowed I was back. He helped unload my gear, then we went inside. The second time he looked out the winder, I asked what had him spooked.

"'I ain't spooked,' he said.

"'Then sit your ass down and drink.'

"He nodded toward headlights up the road, stopped. They hadn't been there five minutes earlier. Then I noticed the pistol sticking from your Pop's waistbelt.

"'Let's see what the hell they want,' I said.

"'Give it a minute. Cut your lights off.'

"I hit the switch, and we stood in the dark, looking at them headlights. They was up yonder"—Marlon pointed with his two fingers holding the cigarette—"at the edge of the woods. Your daddy asked for a smoke, but I told him a deadeye could pop that cherry from five hundred yards. Then them headlights went out.

"'What the shit?' I said.

"'They followed me.'

"I couldn't see your Pop's face—just his silhouette leaning against the wall.

"'How about that drink?' he said.

"He pulled a chair by the winder, set his pistol on the table, then downed the whiskey. I poured another. The road stayed dark. After a while, a truck passed my house, and its brake lights glowed as it stopped beside the car. Then it rounded the curve. A few minutes later, headlights come from the opposite direction, and when the truck poked past my trailer, I seen it was the man who lives near my mama. He drove on.

"'Never knowed you to crawfish from a fight,' I said.

"'They ain't here to fight.'

"I left the room and come back with my .16 gauge and reached for the doorknob when that truck passed the house again. Your Pop grabbed my arm and pointed. This time the car was gone. I sat in a chair and laid the shotgun across my lap.

"We was quiet for a bit. He stared out the winder and drunk straight from the bottle, then he looked at me sidewise. 'I done something.'

"Now, your Pop had done plenty, so when he said he done *something*, I scooted forward.

"He said several years ago he had fooled around with some girl in a barn—a young girl—but nobody knowed. And until they planted her book in his truck that night, he hadn't realized the folks hounding him was connected to the girl. That got your Pop's attention. He knowed she had left a clue in the book to help them piece everything together, so he had thumbed through it and found a marked page—with a heart drawed on it."

Marlon seen he had struck a chord.

"What kind of heart?"

"How many kinds are they?" Marlon grinned and smoked. Then his eyes went distant again as he stared toward the curve. "That girl," he said, "she's God's gift to the devil."

A few days ago, I had walked with Katheryn in the Weldon's backyard after Tammy had cooked dinner. They had an old barn in their field with a sagging roof. Then I remembered how Katheryn hadn't stood in line to speak to Mamma at the funeral home. My stomach jumped.

I had tons of questions, but I hadn't wanted to break Marlon's train of thought—or maybe I feared the answers. But as he fired up a cigarette, my mind flashed to Katheryn and Pop in the Weldon barn.

"Who was the girl?" My voice cracked.

Marlon scratched the back of his head. "At first, I figured your daddy's secret gnawed at him, but regret and your Pop was strangers. So I decided he was putting my nose on the trail in case things turned sideways. But when I asked who was following him, he run his hand along his face. Then he said, 'I ain't gettin' you involved'. I told him it was too late for that, but your daddy was a stubborn mule. He knowed they was biding time. He wasn't afraid, just alert. Seen it plenty."

My mind run full throttle. I wondered how Pop and the girl had met, when they had snuck off together, and how many times he had cheated on Mamma. I thought of Katheryn again. My heart raced.

"Did he"—I couldn't say it, so I changed the word—"*make* her do it?"

"That's just the thing. Your daddy said she come onto him. But he knowed the folks in that car seen it different." Marlon blowed a cloud of smoke.

I remembered Katheryn shifting from foot to foot and how she had blushed as we spoke. I also recalled how Billie Sue had pulled the wool over my eyes.

"Who was in the car?"

He shrugged. "Maybe her brother. Or father. Or grandfather. Hell, maybe all of 'em."

I asked how we could settle the score if he didn't know who it was.

"When my neighbor had stopped beside the car to see if they needed help, they said they was fine, so he doubled back and got the plate. Told me the next day. Said he would've told me then, but my lights was out. He didn't get a clean look, but he seen four men." He pressed his boot on the cigarette in the dirt and lit another. "We find the car, we find the killers."

I wondered if Mr. Weldon and David had been in the car—and what it would do to Mamma and Tammy's friendship. Then Katheryn and her colored heart come to mind. No way in hell, I thought.

"What girl?" I squeezed my hands into fists.

"Your Pop never told me. But I stitched it together." Marlon said the girl's name, then grinned.

"Lois Milford?" My fists opened, and I felt my chest rise and fall. "Don't know no Lois Milford."

"She don't live here." He took a deep drag. "But her mama was a Sumner."

My jaw clinched.

"Hit the nail on the head there, didn't I?"

He *had* hit the nail on the head, and "Sumner" rung like a shot in my ears.

I remembered Savannah glowing in the sun, cupping her hand on her brow. But that image shifted, and I seen her shiny hair tangled with straw, her eyes rolled back, her body thrusted. Her dress was wadded in the dust, and dirt stuck to her sweaty skin as her smooth legs locked around Pop. Then I pictured Savannah and Pop everywhere—in the barn, in the field, beside the creek—and as I tried to stop the onslaught, I realized them images—both true and untrue— had power to haunt.

I had hated Pop at times, but when he had hit me, I hadn't been strong enough to hurt him, and I hadn't been strong enough to pull the trigger like Mamma had done. That shame—the shame for being hit and the shame for not pulling the trigger—had eaten at me for a long time. But as I had watched the McBryars over the years—the way Conley treated Nadine, how he treated Brody—I had a better understanding of what Pop had done to me and Mamma, and I hadn't forgiven him until he died.

But when Marlon mentioned Savannah, my blood boiled again. I seen myself drenched on the Sumner porch, staring past the brown grass and rusted barbwire. I marched across the field in the downpour, busted in the barn, and grabbed a pitchfork.

I tried to rein in my thoughts, but the only thing that helped was believing it couldn't be true: The Sumners wasn't killers, and Pop hadn't touched Savannah.

"Pop lied through his teeth. A pretty girl like that would never want an old man like him."

"I've screwed women I had no business screwin'," Marlon said, "and I've had women turn me down who had no business turnin' me down."

His grin ticked me off. "She wasn't no woman!" Without thinking, I stepped forward.

Quick as lightning, Marlon took a half-step back and flung up his arm, ready to block a punch. I seen the whites of his eyes—but it wasn't fear.

"Easy, son. I'm on your side." His cigarette had fallen from his mouth when he had stepped back. Under his breath, he said, "Goddammit," and picked it up, eyeing me. He blowed dirt off and kept smoking.

I supposed if anyone had been watching they would've had a hard time figuring who was more crazy: Marlon or the Hartline boy who wanted to fight him.

He flicked ash on the ground, and as I looked at the scattered cigarette butts, my blood cooled. I was glad I had caught myself—and grateful the girl hadn't been Katheryn.

I was itching to leave, but I had one burning question. "Why do you care so much?"

The wrinkles around Marlon's eyes disappeared, like he went from staring toward the sun to standing in the shade. "Donny was a good friend. My only friend—at least here anyways." His eyes glassed over. "My father loved your Pop, and your daddy always looked out for my mama. That's a debt I can never repay."

I had been more prepared to hear about Savannah than see Marlon get emotional about Pop.

Marlon exhaled smoke through his nose. "Besides," he said, "I know what it's like to have your daddy killed and never learn who done it." He dropped the cigarette. "If I'd walked to that car when I had the chance, your Pop would still be alive. Wasn't nothing for us to be outnumbered." His mouth twitched.

As he stared toward the curve, I noticed the veins in his folded arms. I wondered when him and Pop had been outnumbered, and I suddenly wanted to hear more.

"Well," he said, "best get back at it." He reached in his pocket, then handed me a piece of paper with a phone number. "Like I said, knowed you was coming." His eyes focused. "Whatever you decide, count me in."

Marlon strode to the lawnmower and tugged the cord. As the mower hummed, I thought it was strange Pop had never mentioned him, and I couldn't understand why Pop had kept so much of himself tucked away.

Driving down the road, I tried to wrap my mind around the connection between Savannah, Mr. Sumner, and Pop's death. Mr. Sumner was a good, Christian man. He wouldn't murder Pop—no matter what Pop had done. Then I considered my anger over Savannah and how much worse it would be for family. I wondered how old her brothers was, and I recalled the two boys at the filling station, poking that stick in the dirt.

I slowed in front of Mrs. Buffington's house. Her grass was trim. I remembered her pointing up the road toward Marlon's, how dingy her living room had seemed as I had glanced over her shoulder, and not knowing what to say when she had told me I favored my father. Then two thoughts met at a crossroads—Pop taking care of Mrs. Buffington, and Pop taking advantage of Savannah—and I stumbled between wishing I had been the one who had shot Pop and wanting to learn what had made him tick.

I heard metal tap glass.

"Well?" Mamma said. She set the spoon on the table and sipped her coffee.

The look in Mamma's eyes reminded me of when I had carried Jake in the woods to put him down. As I had stroked his fur beside his grave, he must've sensed something was different, but he had no way of knowing what was about to happen—or how much I dreaded doing it.

I stared at the reflection of light on the table. Them images of Savannah and Pop had been branded on my brain, and as they run through my mind like wildfire, I knew I couldn't spread it to Mamma. But I couldn't lie to her neither. I thought about what she had endured with Pop and how she was still the most caring person I knew. Then it struck me: Pop had been dealt the winning hand but had cheated anyway.

"You was right," I finally said, meeting her eyes again. "Pop gambled big and lost."

Abigail VIII

Promising Rain

"Greg said he hasn't ruled out murder."

Jesse jerked his head toward me. "Murder?"

"Apparently, he found a clue that could connect it to Jim's death."

"What kind of clue? A casing?"

"He wouldn't say. But I doubt it. She was hung, not shot."

"I was thinking . . . Forget it. You're right."

He turned a hamburger patty, the grease sizzling when it dripped on hot charcoal.

"Greg also said he found one of her mother's old diaries. He didn't know if it had somehow survived in the barn all those years or if she brought it."

"Why would she bring a diary?"

"I couldn't say, but I wouldn't want someone reading about me after I'm gone."

Jesse grinned. "You got a big secret?"

My mind flashed to being crumpled on Donny's kitchen floor the first time he hit me. "Almost."

He cocked his head a second, then finished flipping the patties.

I waved smoke from my face. "Such a selfish thing to do—leaving Gladdis stuck to raise those two children."

Jesse paused and looked at me sideways. "How old?"

"At least eighty."

"I mean the kids."

"Not old enough to drive. Gladdis wags them around everywhere."

He squinted and backed from the smoke.

"Why would she do it?"

Jesse shook his head. "I don't know, Mamma."

As Jesse stared at the burgers, Jack ran up and told us to watch him do a summersault. He pronounced his R's like W's, and I smiled at how he had said it.

"Stay back from the grill," I said.

He kept yelling for his daddy.

"Jesse, Jack's calling you."

"Hm? Oh. I'm watching."

Jack tumbled along the ground. I clapped as he bowed.

"Where's your other shoe?"

"Huh?"

"Sir."

"Sir?"

"You're only wearing one shoe."

Jack looked at his feet, then shrugged. "Weckon I wost it."

"You reckon?"

"Yeah."

"Yes sir."

"Yes sir."

"Where it is?"

"If I knowed where it was, it wouldn't be wost." Jack stared at his father with wide eyes and grubby face. I bit my lip.

Jesse pointed the spatula. "Find it."

When Jack skipped away, I laughed.

"What's so funny?" Katheryn said. She had carried a tray from the house.

I told her.

"How could he not realize he lost a shoe?" Jesse backed from the heat. "Shoes are expensive."

Katheryn wrapped her arm around his waist. "Good thing you're the new foreman. Besides, if he doesn't find it, we can buy one for half price." She smiled.

"Found it!"

We looked toward Jack.

"If that shoe gets holes in it—"

"Then he'll wear a shoe with holes in it," Katheryn said.

Chloe crossed the yard, holding a bouquet of wildflowers she had picked in the field. She ignored her brother and the dog.

"Happy birthday, Grandma!" She handed me the flowers.

"Thank you, sweetheart. They're beautiful!"

I smelled them. It had taken a long time before I could see wildflowers without feeling hollow in my stomach. But I had finally given all that over to God, and the flowers really did bring joy. I marveled at how my happiest days should come at this stage of life.

"Are we celebrating my birthday or your father's promotion?"

"*My* birfday!" Jack said. He was sitting on the ground, making his second attempt to tie his shoe.

Chloe rolled her eyes at him. Then she pinched her chin, pretending to think. "Let's do both."

"That's my girl!" Jesse said. "Want to eat outside?"

I nodded. "It's cooling off." I glanced at the clouds stretching across the sky, hoping it would finally rain.

"We'll set the picnic table," Katheryn said. "Chloe, take the flowers from Grandma and put them in a vase. Who wants sweet tea, and who wants water?"

"How 'bout a Coke?" Jack said.

"You're drinking water, young man." Jack pouted, and Katheryn softened her tone. "Come with me. We need to wash your face before CeCe and Pops get here." She gave me the tray, then took Jack's hand, leading him toward the house.

When they were out of earshot, Jesse said, "Did the sheriff know anything else?".

"He said the coroner confirmed she had been dead two weeks."

"So it took another week until the paper got ahold of it?"

"Greg asked Charlie not to run the story at first. I'm sure Gladdis was a nervous wreck." I held the tray behind my back, tapping it against my arms. "Imagine the rumors I'd hear if I worked at the diner."

Jesse stepped to the grill. "Wasted beauty."

I asked what he meant.

"Beauty is wasted on a girl like that."

"Did you know her?"

"I seen her at the filling station with Mr. Sumner." Jesse placed a slice of cheese on all but Jack's burger. "We was the same age."

"You don't say." I watched smoke from the grill. "Poor Gladdis. Hasn't she been through enough?"

When Jim had died, my heart had finally warmed toward Gladdis. Jim had been killed the same year as Donny, and she had gone to live with Amy in Savannah. I didn't blame her. If I had witnessed my husband's murder, I wouldn't have stayed in that house either.

Then I thought about how last month the local newspaper had published Amy's obituary. It hadn't mentioned the cause of death, but I had heard she had been in a sanitorium.

After Gladdis had moved, her home had remained empty for over ten years. I didn't know if she chose not to sell the property or if it was because people claimed the house was haunted. I couldn't speak for the house, but the family seemed cursed: One of Amy's sons lost his leg from infection after a hunting accident, Jim was shot in his own kitchen, and Amy died at sixty—an age I used to consider ancient. Now, not two months later, I was glad Amy hadn't lived to learn her only daughter had hung herself in their old barn. But Gladdis, on the other hand . . . How could one person endure such loss, I thought.

I recalled the creases at the corners of her mouth during Jim's funeral. I had never wanted to hug someone so much in my life. I wondered if I should drive to Savannah for her granddaughter's service.

"Mamma?"

Jesse balanced a patty on the spatula, waiting for me to hold the tray level. After he piled the burgers on it, I laid the tray beside the baked beans and potato salad. I spread tinfoil over the meat and covered the bowls with napkins. Chloe had set the plates, and Katheryn brought two pitchers and poured drinks.

As Tammy and Darrell came around the side of the house, Jack burst out the door.

"Pops!"

"Hey, little buddy!"

Jack leaped in Darrell's arms. His face was clean, but his shoelace dangled.

I hugged Tammy. "I didn't hear you pull up."

She handed me a gift. "It's nothing, but it reminded me of you."

I read the card and opened the present. "It's perfect!" The magnet showed a steaming mug of coffee stamped with Philippians 4:13.

Chloe stepped outside with silverware bundled in her hand and kissed her grandparents on the cheek.

"What a pretty dress!" Tammy said.

Chloe thanked her, and after she arranged the silverware, I asked her to stick the magnet on the refrigerator and display the card with the others—including a playful card Conley and Nadine had sent and a touching one from Jackie and Dewayne, who had inserted a picture of their teenagers.

I tied Jack's shoe before Darrell put him down, then we all walked to the table. They made me sit at the head.

Jack peeked while Jesse said grace.

After Donny died, Jesse had stayed in town a couple of weeks to help me settle into my new life. He had gathered Donny's tools from the shop, finished repairing the neighbor's car Donny had been working on in our yard, and met Marlon.

Jesse hadn't told me everything he had learned from Marlon, but he had told me enough. Several days afterwards, when I had served Greg at the diner, I had gone to the parking lot with him and asked who Donny had been mixed up with. Greg had jingled change in his pocket and said it could have been any number of folks, and how whoever had killed Donny had covered their tracks.

It sickened me whenever my mind wandered to Donny's final moments. Had he been frightened? Had he known he would die? Had he thought of me?

I sometimes wondered what I would do if I knew who had killed him.

After Jesse had talked with Marlon, he and I had visited Jefferey's office. He had drafted new paperwork for the house and property, removing Donny's name and adding Jesse's. I had appreciated Jefferey's help, but I had felt awkward and glanced down when he had grinned at me.

He couldn't seem to understand I needed time to mourn—even after everything Donny had put me through—and over the next few months, he had pressured me for a relationship. Jefferey had said he missed our phone conversations, then laughed about hanging up on Donny whenever he had answered. At the time, I still hadn't overcome the guilt of having feelings for another man behind Donny's back, and I had bristled at the thought of what Jefferey had said at visitation. And since he had wanted all or nothing, our friendship had ended. I couldn't comprehend how he was prepared to either spend the rest of his life with me or wash his hands of me. Then, within six months, he became engaged. I wondered if he had courted her while wooing me, and I suspected—after his long separation and messy divorce—he had just wanted a housewife.

Shortly after Jefferey's engagement, George McCullough had asked me to dinner. Although I had been hesitant because of our age difference, I had accepted—but I never developed romantic feelings and told him we made better friends than lovers. He had looked disappointed at first, then smiled and said he was a bit rusty when it came to dating anyway. We had remained close until he had passed away two years ago.

But even though I sometimes got the blues living alone, the Lord had a plan. If I had remarried, Jesse, Katheryn, Chloe, and Jack wouldn't have moved in after I broke my collarbone, and the pain from my fall was worth the joy I received from having loved ones sleeping under my roof again.

Were it not for Tammy, I would never have known Jesse and Katheryn had written letters following his return to Cullman. Letters had evolved to phone calls, and a year after Donny died, Jesse had come home and bought a small house with money he had earned from Conley. He and Katheryn had dated several months. Their wedding was one of the greatest moments of my life.

Billy Tucker had happily rehired Jesse, and with everything Conley had taught him about sawmills, he had worked his way up the ladder. And now that Billy had retired, Jesse had been promoted to foreman. Linda had quit after she and Billy had separated, and Katheryn had replaced her, which meant I watched Jack during the day and was home for Chloe when the school bus dropped her off in the afternoon. Jack was a handful, but he made up for it with his affection.

I wondered how Donny had influenced the way Jesse raised his children. They knew when he meant business, but he never spanked them. Chloe liked to read to him, and Jack always wanted to play rodeo. On his hands and knees, Jesse pretended to be the bull, and when he threw Jack, he would bellow and shake his head in Jack's belly, making him giggle until he was breathless. Even after a hard day of work, he played with the children—down on the floor or outdoors in the dirt—the way Donny had done on his good days.

Sometimes, it seemed a lifetime ago when I last saw my husband. But some mornings when I awoke, I reached for him. I remembered how we enjoyed relaxing on the swing in the evenings—and how comforting it was to nestle into his side. And I remembered the way his eyes crinkled when I hit a target, then blew gunsmoke from the barrel.

I still kept his pistol in my nightstand.

Now, sitting beneath open sky and surrounded by cherished family, I rested my clasped hands on the edge of the table, blessed beyond measure.

Far away, thunder rumbled.

"We'd best cut the cake inside," Katheryn said. Everyone but Jack gathered dishes and hurried toward the house. Chloe chased a napkin that had blown from her plate.

"C'mon, Gwandma! We're gonna sing to you!" Jack grabbed my hand and pulled.

"Run along, child. I'll be right there."

I looked to the heavens. The day had been hot, but the shifting clouds were dark grey, promising rain, and the breeze cooled me. I felt the first sprinkle and smiled. After a long, dry summer, rains were good for soothing the soul—and for laying autumn's dust.

The distant, rolling thunder reminded me of unseen power. I closed my eyes and—hands uplifted—hummed my favorite hymn.

Donny VIII

The Bones of Secrets

The alcohol smelt pretty loud as I come to. I blinked to make sure my eyes was open, but everything stayed black. My left arm tingled, and rope bound my wrists in front of me. What the hell, I thought. Then I felt movement and heard the engine. We hit a bump, and bottles clinked in the wooden box scraping my back. I could tell they was full.

I pushed my feet against the inside of the trunk but couldn't straighten my legs. I was missing a boot. I raised my wrists to my teeth and bit at the knot, working it loose enough to get blood flowing and free my hand when the time come. I opened and closed my fingers until I had pricks of feeling.

The road growed rougher, and the car slowed and splashed through potholes. I wondered how far that bootlegger had brung me.

Now and again, I heard muffled voices, but I knowed at least one of them fellas wouldn't be too chatty for a while. The back of my head burned, and I reached up and rubbed the knot on my skull. I hadn't had my bell rung like that in years. That split second was all they needed, I thought. Should've kept moving.

After I had left Marlon's, I had took the long way home to watch if I was tailed. The moon was so bright I could've drove without lights. I doubled back to the garage and didn't see nothing, so I headed to the house. Just shy of the crossroads, I seen a car pull out behind me. I sped up, and it clung to my bumper. I kept one hand on the wheel and gripped my pistol with the other. At the crossroads, I gunned the engine and hit the dip where blacktop met dirt. When them headlights faded at the stop sign and the car turned, I knowed my imagination had got the better of me. I laid my pistol on the seat.

A few miles later, I rounded the curve at Wilson's Crook and stood on them binders with both feet to keep from bulldozing a tree laying across the road. The .45 thudded in the floor as I slid to a stop. Dust swallered the truck and glowed in my headlights. As the dust thinned, I noticed a vehicle parked on the other side of the tree. Then its lights come on, blinding me. I reached down, groping for my gun.

Someone flung my door open, grabbing at me, and I stretched across the seat and put the boots to him while feeling along the floorboard. He clamped one of my ankles between his arm and ribcage, and that boot slipped off when I reared my leg back, then my other bootheel nailed him square in the jaw. He staggered back, but two men took his place, filling that doorway. One clutched the cuff of my britches. As they dragged me out, my fingers wrapped around metal, and I jumped up swinging that tire iron. Them two boys was on the ground in a jiffy. Then a car pulled behind my truck. All four doors opened, and—

*

So now I laid in that trunk, pumping my hands, second-guessing myself. I knowed Wilson's Crook better than anybody, and I could've lost them blockheads at the water runoff of Bobcat Bluff. But I had never dodged a fight—no matter the odds. Abigail had called it a flaw—she pointed out all mine—but this time she weren't too far from plumb.

She'd've questioned my decision not to involve Marlon too. If he had been with me, we could've handled them boys, easy. But Marlon had enough trouble without collecting more enemies, so I hadn't let him walk out to that car, toting that shotgun. Now, I wished I hadn't mentioned that girl neither.

That girl, I thought. The she-devil. I remembered her leaning over the loft rail and blowing them daisy petals from her cupped hands, and I recalled the underlined name in the dirt, the page she marked, and the heart above her handwriting in the book: *In your arms, I was always Lolita.* But the bones of secrets eventually get plowed up, and I knowed I had made two mistakes: Handing Gladdis that book, and not burning that goddamn house to the ground.

The car hit another bump, and I rocked into the box again. Them bottles rattled.

I had left the book with Marlon, but I wondered if Abigail would learn about that girl another way—or if she'd know my restless nights on the cot was to keep her safe. But I doubted she'd admit nothing I done was for the good of family. She frowned on my methods, but I had taught her to stand up for herself, and our son was a man because of me. I remembered Jesse's muscles flexing when he split firewood, and how good he become at tackling. Still, he was as bitter as Abigail.

Yesterday, I had told Mrs. Buffington how Jesse hung up whenever I answered the phone. She had said he needed more time, but after a half-dozen years, I weren't so sure.

Then she had asked about Abigail.

"She's fine."

We usually left it there, but Mrs. Buffington said, "When was the last time you and Abigail did something fun together?".

Me and Abigail was only together when we ate or watched TV. We never talked, we never touched, and she still slept in Jesse's room. I had tried smoothing things over, but forgiveness was a hammer she only swung at church.

I slowly shook my head. "Couldn't say."

"I remember how excited you were about dating her."

Mrs. Buffington started to say something else, then hesitated. We was sitting in her living-room chairs, facing the broad window. Across her front yard, she had a view of the road. I wondered how many cars she counted daily.

"When Stanley died," she finally said, "I didn't have the chance to say goodbye. I don't even know what we discussed at breakfast." She wiped her eyes. "Before leaving for work, he kissed me at the door, and I watched him drive away. How could I have known I wouldn't see him again?"

I should've said something, but I couldn't talk about that day without my eyes burning.

"I think about Stanley, and I'm grateful for our time together. But I think just as much about the time stolen from us."

She stared straight ahead. She had never sounded sorry for herself before, and I wondered when it had took root. Mr. Buffington had been my age when he died—over twenty years ago. Twenty years, I thought. Damnation. He had been dead as many years as they had been married.

"Was y'all always happy?"

"We never had a cross word." She smiled. "But sometimes a slammed cabinet door and a cold shoulder speak louder than words."

I considered how Abigail banged dishes or stomped down the hall.

"But you can't always get your way in marriage," Mrs. Buffington said, "and compromise is the salve that heals resentment."

"I wouldn't've figured y'all got mad at each other."

"Everyone's path gets rocky. But our experiences— good and bad—are the ingredients that make us who we are." She leaned toward me. "Give me your hand."

I stretched my arm across the small, round table between us. She run her fingertips along my palm. Chills shot up my arm, and I couldn't recall the last time I had been touched.

"Why do you have this scar?"

"Got cut."

"That's the answer of a simple man."

"I am a simple man."

She patted my hand. "That scar is a reminder good can come from evil. The Lord brought you into my life through sin. At the time, I assumed it was for your benefit, but over the years, I learned it was for mine. So the Lord has always been working in both our lives."

"Maybe he's like me. The harder he works, the worse things get."

She snapped her head toward me. "Don't make light of the Lord!"

I wanted to crawl under the chair. She hadn't give me that look since I was a teenager, and I had never cussed in front of her again.

"What I mean," I said, "is sometimes carving out a living ain't enough."

I knowed I had squandered money, but I also knowed honest living didn't always pay, and I recalled standing in Jim's kitchen, holding that wad of cash.

"The Lord is testing you."

"Flunked ever' test I ever took."

I expected her to scold me again, but she said, "This one isn't over".

A truck I didn't recognize drove down the road.

"I worry about you," she said, like she had read my mind. "And sitting in this quiet house, I have a lot of time to worry—about you, about Marlon." She took a deep breath. "I'd be lost without the two of you."

"I never knowed a stronger woman. You'd get by."

"Getting by isn't living, and I get by plenty."

I looked at her, not sure what to say. I imagined her days was long and lonely as she stared out the window, waiting.

She rested her wrinkled, yellow hands in her lap. Her fingers curled inward, the joints knotted. I remembered how gently those hands had held mine when she had peeled back the bloodstained cloth, and how I had sat up straight when she had cleaned and bandaged my cut. And I remembered her soft lips kissing me on the forehead after she had finished.

I run my thumb over my scar, thinking I should visit more often, when my stomach jolted. "I just realized the date."

She nodded, her mouth tight.

I couldn't speak for a stretch. I wanted to hug her.

Not until later, after pulling my boots on, did brightness show in her eyes again.

"I appreciate you mowing my yard today," she said, standing at the door with a brown bag. The top was folded. "I wish you'd take money."

"Them cookies is pay enough."

At the bottom of the steps, I recalled what she had said about Mr. Buffington. I turned. "I love you."

Tears welled up in her eyes. "You are my second son, Donny Hartline."

As I drove away, she watched from the door.

Now, in that trunk, worrying about Mrs. Buffington, I feared death for the first time in my life.

Brakes squeaked, and the car stopped. About eight doors shut. Voices blended, and dogs barked. Someone laughed. The engine clicked as it cooled, then I heard footsteps followed by the key sliding in the lock. The decklid popped open, and they hauled me out and shoved me on the ground. The damp dirt felt cold. Two men hefted me to my knees.

I squinted against the glare. When my eyes adjusted, I knowed the headlights was from a pair of trucks. I seen four people's silhouettes, and a man I didn't recognize stood beside me with a shotgun.

They had brung me to a clearing surrounded by woods, and I knelt next to a wide puddle. Tires had rutted the ground. The moon was high now, and as I gauged the distance to them trees, an owl screeched.

A man fetched that box from the car trunk and lugged it between the trucks. I heard the box grate across the bed, then the tailgate slammed. Them dogs whined and scratched at their kennel.

When the man stepped into the light, he held a jug.

"Hold off the libation," a familiar voice said.

He set that jug down.

A figure broke from the shadow and strode toward me. He wore a brimmed hat.

"I didn't think—"

Somebody kicked me in the back of the ribs, and I fell sideways in the mudpuddle. The man with the shotgun pressed his bootheel on my temple, then shifted more weight to the boot. My head slowly sunk in mud to where my nose and mouth was at the surface. When I gulped water down my windpipe, I jerked my head from beneath that boot and spat, coughing. I pushed myself to my knees. I felt grit between my teeth.

"Don't kill him yet. Hell, he might miss the point."

Men laughed.

My clothes was soaked, and mud squished between the toes of my naked foot. Water dripped down my face. From the corner of my eye, I seen the man cradling that shotgun in the crook of his arm.

"Know why you're here?" Jim asked.

I dug my toes deeper in the cool mud.

"Some might call it revenge," Jim said. "Some might call it a reckoning. And some might even call it a come-to-Jesus. But since the wife can't abide blasphemy, I call it good old-fashioned justice." He stretched his arm to the side. "And my friend with the badge agrees."

I looked in the direction Jim pointed and seen the outline of a holster hanging at the man's hip. Jim might've been bluffing, but if the law was there, I'd lay odds who it was.

"Don't get me wrong,"—Jim throwed his hand up and waved it—"I love me some Jesus!"

"Amen, brother," someone said.

"But I'm an Old Testament man. 'Thou shalt' this, 'Thou shalt not' that. Hell, just today I heard my new favorite passage: 'There shalt be heaviness and sorrow and thou shalt be brought down and thy speech shall whisper out of the dust'."

He paused, and I caught a glimpse of his smirk. I grinded that grit between my teeth again. I wondered how often Abigail's forked tongue had poisoned Jim's ear, and I now knowed the blood of Judas run in her veins.

"It's a pow'rful verse," Jim said. "But when I cracked open the Good Book, guess what I discovered. It's a misquote. Some information is omitted." He hung his thumbs on his belt. "That means left out."

Jim give his congregation time to react. But I'd bet the ones who laughed loudest hadn't knowed what it meant neither.

"You could argue," Jim said, "the omitted information isn't important. But you could also argue by leavin' out information you alter the nature of the passage. It's all about interpretation. And what we tell ourselves about our interpretations is how we live with ourselves after our actions."

He pulled out a handkerchief and wiped his face. I had heard different ideas on how Jim had come by his money, but they all amounted to the same thing: He drove more crooked roads than I ever done. But there he stood, like a preacher at revival, washed in the blood.

"Who among us hasn't heard 'an eye for an eye'?" Jim looked side to side as he folded the handkerchief and slid it in his pocket. He adjusted his hat. "My grandbaby changed after that summer you lurked in my barn. The wife always had her suspicions—women's intuition, we'll call it—but that novel finally provided proof of your transgressions."

He stepped forward, and even in that lighting, I could tell his eyes narrowed.

"So I come to my point, Donny. When you raped my grandbaby, you took more than an eye."

"I didn't rape nobody!"

The butt of that shotgun walloped my skull, and I splashed in the mudpuddle. I spat and straightened to my knees again. Water trickled from my hair. My ear rung.

I wondered if what Jim said was true. Then I considered his comment on interpretation. Maybe the girl *had* changed, but maybe she had become exactly what she wanted—and he just didn't like it.

"My Pappy had a sayin'," Jim said. "'When the devil steals the angel's share, there will be hell to pay'." He clucked his tongue. "Now," he said, lifting a finger, "you have permission to speak. Better make it enlightening."

I looked past Jim. I still couldn't tell their number, but two men had my attention—the man with the holster, and the one propped against the hood of a truck with his heel resting on the bumper, holding a rifle upright on his thigh.

I cleared my throat, then spoke loud. "The wages of sin is death."

"That's right, Donny," Jim said. "Eat some crow." I heard a few chuckles.

I leveled my eyes at Jim. "But the sin was worth it." I slipped one hand from the rope and whipped my left leg up, pushing off to the side and ramming my shoulder into the man who stood over me. He sprawled on the ground, dropping that shotgun. I grabbed it by the barrel and planted the butt of the gun in his teeth, then swung it around and shot from the hip on the run. I emptied both barrels in Jim's direction. Someone screamed. Them dogs started yapping. I slung the gun aside and sprinted for the trees. Shots rung out, and bullets sliced past me.

I dove behind the first trunk and peeked around it, sucking wind. Men scurried in the headlights, and somebody laid on the ground with shadows hunched over him. A silhouette stood in the field, rifle raised. The muzzle flashed, and a bullet ricocheted through the woods.

I turned, hotfooting it. The tree canopies blocked most of the moonlight, and all I seen was black boles. I shielded my face with my arm, branches slapping against it.

I forgot I was missing a boot until I stubbed my toe and stumbled. My elbow smashed the ground, and something scraped my forearm, but I hopped up, listening. The yells sounded distant, but the barking had growed louder. I wished I'd've kept that shotgun.

I raked my fingers along the underbrush for something to club them dogs with—then sprung up. The sound of running water had appeared from thin air. I hustled toward it.

At the bank, I doubled over with my hands on my knees, my head dizzy. A river, I thought. Where the hell am I?

Suddenly, my arm pulsed with raw pain. I reached over and felt something slick on my skin, then my thumb found the gash.

As I peeled off my wet shirt and wrapped my forearm, I remembered Marlon telling me about being stabbed but not feeling it until after he had killt the man who done it. Then I remembered him wearing that green coat in the liquor store, all teeth as he rubbed his buzzed hair. Years later, Mrs. Buffington had told me Marlon had returned home a different man, but I couldn't have said—I just knowed I never seen that big smile again.

Then another smile come to mind, and I pictured that girl wading in the creek—raising her eyes to mine, holding the sides of her dress—and none of it seemed real—the girl, the book, shooting at Jim.

The landscape spun. My arm throbbed. As the spinning slowed to a stop, I studied the river. The rapids glowed white, and a dark pool spread below the chutes. Then more white.

I glanced back and seen shadows gliding through the trees. The roar had muffled the barking, but them dogs had reeled me in. I hoped they was timid of swuft water.

Fording the river, I was thigh-deep in three steps, my feet sliding over smooth stones. Halfway across, I leaned into the water breaking against my hip when my boot slipped. The current swept me downstream. I banged against a boulder and clawed at it, but my fingers couldn't find purchase. Then the rapids dumped me into the pool. Everything went black.

My head resurfaced, and even with an earful of river, I could tell them dogs had changed their pitch. Someone hollered, and guns fired. Bullets zipped overhead. Moonlight caught a splash between me and the bank as I drifted toward the next run of chutes.

The heavy shirt created drag, but I ducked underwater and swum in darkness. When I come up for air, I knowed I'd reach the other side before getting sucked down them rapids. My toes touched bottom. I focused on the riverbank, and as I searched for footing, random images flashed through my mind: The busted bottle in the liquor store, my pistol in Abigail's hands, Amy in the barn. Another bullet splashed in front of me, and I thought about Jesse and that girl. And how they was the same age. Then a thought struck me that made my stomach jolt, and I wondered if—

Jesse IX

The Lean Shadows of Autumn

I was laying in bed, trying to recapture the smell of bacon that had disappeared in the half-light of dawn, and I rolled to my back. I couldn't remain in one spot without aching. I would adjust all night, shifting pain from my shoulders to my back or hips—until I growed tired of searching for the right position and got up. Some mornings, my neck had a crook in it.

I slid from the covers and sat on the edge of the bed, elbows on my thighs. "Eight long years," I said, and hardly believed it. I rested my face in my hands.

Katheryn died eight years ago today, shortly after turning sixty-two. Autumn had always been my favorite season—cooler weather, changing leaves, football—but after Katheryn passed, I had realized autumn was slow death.

I used to take flowers to her grave, but I hated thinking of her sealed in a casket underground, so I hadn't visited the cemetery in years. I figured it wouldn't be long until I was laying beside her nohow—or so I hoped. I had never feared dying too young, but I had growed afraid of living too old.

I recalled how, as a teenager, I had recognized family names in the cemetery but hadn't knowed no one buried there. Now, I knew too many—including myself since both our names was etched on Katheryn's tombstone. My side just lacked a date.

I thought about how hayrides used to drive through the graveyard around Halloween, but, last week, no wagons or trucks full of rowdy kids had passed the house. They probably didn't do that stuff nowadays, but we used to laugh, cut up, and tell ghost stories on them hayrides. I remembered the time Evan ribbed me for not kissing Angie Dobbins, and how, that next weekend, he had conned buddies into rigging a rope around Tommy Williams, so it had looked like he had been hung from the oak tree in the middle of the cemetery.

Then I thought about how Savannah had hung herself for real, and how she had rotted for two weeks before the sheriff found her. I wondered if anyone who had seen Tommy had knowed a person who had hung themself. If so, our gag wouldn't have been funny to them.

But outside of experience, understanding drawed up short—even for adults. If I had really considered how Nana Beulah had spent her last years following Papa Jacob's death, I would've made the kids stay with her more. But, after living alone eight years, I better understood my grandmother, and I sometimes caught myself talking to Katheryn, or I woke thinking I smelled breakfast, and—for a minute—she was with me. I clung to them moments as long as possible.

I finally stood and pulled the blankets over the pillows, then dressed and started coffee. When I stepped on the porch, Pepper's tail tapped the wood floor a few times—

right near the slabs needing replaced. He slowly stretched, then raised his grey muzzle. The cool air chilled me, and I knew Pepper would need to sleep indoors soon. He used to stay outside all winter. I stooped to pet him. "Let's check on the ladies."

He walked beside me toward the chicken coop. Halfway to the pen, we crossed a small section of wood sorrel amidst the grass. Pop had worked on cars there, and motor oil had seeped into the ground. For a long time, it had been a hard patch of dirt.

"Mornin', ladies." The chickens clucked and scampered out of my path. I set their brown eggs in a bowl. The first couple had rolled around. I thanked them and propped open the gate, so they could peck in the yard during the day. I used to keep Pepper from them, but he had lost interest in chasing hens long ago.

I collected seven eggs each morning, and I placed extras in a carton on the porch rail a few days per week, so Munford could deliver them to the Widow Johnson. She lived with her daughter and son-in-law and their kids, and sometimes the Power Board cut their electricity.

After hobbling up the steps, Pepper laid on the porch, and I knew—one way or another—he would be my last dog.

I left the front door open, and the breeze blowed through the screen door. The dented wiring bulged inward. I cracked two shells on the lip of the frying pan and stretched bacon strips on Mamma's old cast-iron skillet. The eggs hissed as the bacon popped and sizzled. I thought about how

Katheryn had whipped up a big breakfast in no time: biscuits, gravy, eggs, sausage, bacon. I never made a biscuit that touched hers.

I put the bacon and eggs on a plate, then poured coffee and stood at the counter. The golden yolk spread when I pricked it with my fork.

I jumped when the phone rung.

Since no one else called, I knew it was Chloe. She lived in Chattanooga with her husband and three children, so I only seen her once a week.

"Hey, Daddy," Chloe said. "I can't make it today. Samuel is sick and missed school."

"I'm sorry to hear that."

"It's going around real bad. Maggie ran a fever this weekend. Lord help if Michael gets it. He's the worst when he's sick."

Sam cried in the background. "Sounds like somebody's unhappy."

"Right now, we all are. I gotta go, Daddy."

"I'll see you next we—"

I heard the click. I hung up and stared at the phone, wondering if Chloe remembered today was the anniversary of her mother's death. But she had her hands full and probably felt enough guilt for not visiting, so I wouldn't mention it later.

I stepped to the counter. Breakfast was cold.

That little Maggie was something, I thought. She would sit in my lap and jabber up a storm. I reckoned she got that from Katheryn—a grandmother she would never know.

I recalled the last time I heard my wife's voice. After learning she had a week to live, she had decided to die in her own bed. The doctor hadn't liked that idea, but I had told him to go to hell, and I brung Katheryn home.

Chloe saw her every day that week, but Jack didn't come until the funeral. He must've been somewhere doing something more important.

Her last few days, Katheryn didn't eat much and slept most of the time. I took care of her as best I could. I owed her plenty for all them years she had cared for me. But it was hard seeing her so thin and weak, and I never thought about them last days without shedding a tear. A year had passed before I could remember her any other way.

When she was awake, I read to her, or we discussed the kids and grandkids or things we had done. After what we had went through with Granny, I was thankful Katheryn's mind had stayed sharp.

"Remember our fishing trip?" she had said.

I asked how could I forget.

Katheryn had never trout fished, so I had loaded a couple of rods and tackle in the truck, and we drove to Tellico. I could throw a stone across the river in most places, but it had lots of good runs and deep pools. Katheryn had struggled with releasing the cast button, but once she got the hang of it, her lure usually hit the stream.

At one point, I had seen her yanking the rod, trying to free the snagged hook. On the far side, a branch had swung back and forth over the water.

I had splashed toward Katheryn, cut the line with my knife, and pulled her up the bank. After hustling down the road, I had turned and pointed. The branch she had tugged was weighted down with a hornet's nest. A blur had swarmed it. She said she had been too concerned about stepping on a snake to notice the hornets.

We had seen multiple nests that day, and the old-timer at the bait shop had said to expect a mild winter since they was built low over the river. But I forgot if that had held true.

Sitting beside Katheryn's bed, I had pinched the bridge of my nose, then said, "We was lucky we wasn't eat up".

"Like when you bush-hogged? You looked like a wild man running across the field, waving your arms."

She had winced, then covered it with a smile. I had held her near hand, and she had reached with her other one and traced my veins. My skin had wrinkled beneath her touch.

Our last evening together, she had asked me to read the Bible to her, so I had read several of her favorite Psalms. After a while, she stopped me.

"I need you to promise me something—Jesse Hartline."

"Anything."

"Keep going to church, and keep the Faith. I couldn't bear not seeing you again."

She had trembled through teardrops.

"My sweet Katheryn. We'll be together again. I promise."

Her lips had made a thin smile, then she had shut her eyes and drifted to sleep. I had took the bookmark—the tattered crooked heart—from the nightstand, marked Psalms 46, and closed the Bible. I had rested my face in my hands and sat for a long time.

So whenever I heard Maggie chattering, she reminded me of Katheryn, and I figured that was why she was my favorite. Maggie made my old experiences fresh—watching a hummingbird, holding a caterpillar, hearing a whippoorwill. With the rate she talked and her love of nature, she was a perfect mix between Katheryn and Mamma.

I scraped the remainder of breakfast on Pepper's food and placed his dish in front of him. Then I carried my steaming mug to the porch and set it on the small table next to my chair. The crisp air hinted of the first killing frost.

I lit a cigar, then sipped coffee and smoked. At the end of the porch, the swing gently swayed in the breeze. Pepper curled beside me. He had only eaten a few bites too.

Looking over the yard, I wondered if I would rake after all the leaves fell. But judging by the old hickory at the edge of the field, I guessed not. The dead hickory had finally blowed down during the last storm, and I had let it lay for several months. Katheryn would've made me clear that tree the next day. "When I'm gone, don't let our home get run down," she had said. "That McCurdy house has gone to pot since Elaine passed away." But nothing was the same without my bride, and I could clean up the hickory later—or watch it rot.

I remembered how Katheryn had played matchmaker with McCurdy and Rose Blevins after Miss Elaine died. The image of two old people on a date had struck me as funny, and I recalled teasing Mamma about Mr. McCullough. But a few years after Katheryn's death, I learned how McCurdy had felt—not only about letting things get run down, but about somebody wanting to set him up. The preacher had tried to spark interest between me and a widow from church. I had told him the widow wouldn't go for a long tooth, and he had said she wasn't no spring chicken neither. We both had laughed. He had pressed once more. "I appreciate you watching over your flock, Preacher," I had said, "but this old gunslinger has holstered his pistol for good."

Shortly after that conversation, I broke my promise to Katheryn. Folks at church was always curious how I was doing or saying they missed Katheryn or asking about the grandchildren. I supposed they had good intentions, but I growed tired of telling the same people the same thing. And it got to where—other than family—I didn't care to see nobody noway.

But now and then the preacher would stop by. At first, I tolerated it since he had spoke at Katheryn's funeral.

He had told about the time she went to church in her house slippers by mistake. Chloe had never heard that story, and she had squeezed my hand and smiled through tears.

The preacher had persisted with his pop-ins, and after a while, I looked forward to them—and probably enjoyed them more than he done. He knew the Bible better than anybody I ever met, even Mamma. But he didn't say nothing I hadn't heard before, and he couldn't answer my questions—at least, not to my satisfaction. Chances was good everyone else simply agreed with him, and he must've liked the challenge because he kept coming back.

One time, though, I flustered him. I had been reading Revelation and asked about the dragon and the stars. The preacher had shifted in his seat. "Some people think that's true," he had finally said.

"I ain't askin' them."

He moved his Bible from one hand to the other, but to his credit, he answered. "The Scripture supports it, so I believe it too."

"Well, don't that seem like a lot?"

He sat still. "What do you mean?"

"If God created a hundred angels, then Lucifer convinced thirty-three to rebel. How do you reckon that's possible if heaven is all it's cracked up to be?"

The preacher's face went blank, and I was certain Katheryn had rolled over in her grave.

"And if angels fought a war in heaven, how in the world can humans get along?"

He gripped his Bible. "These are tough questions, Jesse,"—It had took about twenty reminders before he had stopped calling me Mr. Hartline—"and my answer is this: I haven't the foggiest idea. But the Lord has his reasons, and we are woefully underqualified to question them."

Over the last couple years, I had read the Bible daily. But the more I learned, the more I realized I didn't know, and I wondered why bother if it only created questions.

"Here's an easier one. What do we tell folks if something sounds too good to be true?"

He sighed, then glanced at the clock. "You've spent a lifetime holding down pews, and I admire how you study—not read, but study—the Bible. But your questions echo the doubt in your heart. So I have one for you now: What do you believe?"

I fidgeted in my chair as much as he had, but I owed him an answer. "My great sin is I don't know what I believe."

The clock tolled the hour.

"With all due respect, Mr. Hartline," he said in his pulpit tone, "at your age, maybe it's better to have more faith and fewer questions."

Not many days went by when I didn't think about what he had said—and I knew he was right.

Even though I gave him a hard time, I was grateful he had tightened the screws on me—especially when I felt low. Me and Katheryn had kept Mamma's .38 in the nightstand, but after Katheryn died, I had moved it under her pillow. On long, dark nights, I slid my hand over and wrapped my fingers around the cold handle. I liked keeping it close—in case I needed it. A couple of times, I thought I might. But when the morning light shone through the window after them black nights, I was always glad I hadn't pulled the trigger.

The pistol hadn't been shot in years, and sometimes I considered putting it back in the drawer—alongside the .300 Win Mag casing, which, for ages, I had kept hidden.

Not long after Mr. Sumner's death, the shiny casing had appeared on my doorstep in Cullman, standing upright. When I had picked it up, I noticed something flush with the edge of the cartridge mouth. I had slipped it out and unrolled the paper: *I don't think no less of you. We ain't all cut out for it.* No one had been arrested for Mr. Sumner's murder, but I knew I had held the smoking gun.

The day before I had returned to Cullman after Pop's funeral, Marlon had come to the house when Mamma had left for the diner. He had asked how we was getting even. But as much as he pushed for revenge, I knew I'd regret it, and somehow our conversation had reminded me of the one with Pop after that football game against Rogers. When Marlon heard I didn't have no plan, I had seen disappointment in his eyes.

Later, after Mamma had told me how Mr. Sumner had died, I had pictured him sitting across from Mrs. Sumner, eating breakfast. Then I wondered if she had been looking at him when his head had exploded, and if chunks of his brain or shards from his skull had splattered on the wall—or her.

Still, even though Marlon had killed Mr. Sumner in cold blood—considering what had happened to Pop—I hadn't thought no less of him neither.

Years later, Mamma had learned Sheriff Castleberry had suspected Marlon murdered both Mr. Sumner and Savannah. I had held my breath when she had mentioned Marlon and Mr. Sumner in the same sentence, but whatever clues the sheriff had found hadn't been enough to press charges.

Marlon was long gone by then anyway. The last time I had seen him was at Mrs. Buffington's funeral, nearly a year after me and Katheryn married. At the graveside, Marlon had gripped my hand.

I had glanced from the pavilion and jutted my chin toward a large headstone marked "Sumner".

"A shame the way he got called home," I had said.

"Ain't it, though?"

He had winked, then turned and spoke to someone. I had stood, thinking about him and Mr. Sumner, and I had wondered how many other hands I had shook with blood on them.

I had stored Marlon's casing in Pop's old toolbox until Katheryn passed. That cartridge—and everything it signified—was the only secret I had kept from my wife.

I puffed my cigar and blowed a smoke ring. I gazed past the dead hickory toward the field. In springtime, the thin wings of insects would catch the slanting rays of the evening sun, and dragonflies would dart back and forth, feasting. Honeysuckle would fill the air, and lightning bugs would glow after sunset. Me and Katheryn used to swing on the porch, watching flashes as the moon rose over the mountain. Now and then, if a firefly flew near, she would reach out. When she opened her hand, it would walk to the tip of her finger, spread its wings for a second, then fly away. Katheryn would smile every time.

But the field wasn't full of life now, and over the last two weeks, the leaves had turned different shades of red and yellow and brown. Everything was dying, which was fine with me. It meant less work, less heat, and less dust.

I compared what little I done to how Chloe stretched herself too thin with raising three kids, volunteering for boards, and teaching Sunday school. I figured Jack stayed just as busy since he never come around. But he lived further off, so I shouldn't hold that against him. I supposed I hadn't been much different when I had moved away, and I felt bad I had left Mamma alone with Pop for so long. But without Cullman, I would've never knowed Conley, and no telling where I would've ended up without his influence. I remembered how he had given me my first cigar, and how I had been nervous to smoke it in front of Mamma.

Now, as I stared at the grey block of ash, that fishing trip come to mind again. After riling up the hornets, we had found a good run, and Katheryn had caught a trout and landed it beside me on the riverbank. As I had removed the barb from the fish's lip, I had accidentally pulled the line. Katheryn had shouted, "I got another one!", then jerked the rod and set the hook—in my thumb. When I hollered, Katheryn had realized what had happened and tried to stifle her laugh but become more tickled. I had finally laughed too. The next time she had landed a fish, I made her drop the rod before removing the hook. She had laughed again.

I tapped the cigar, and the ash fell in the tray.

That crook in my neck flared up. I squeezed and rubbed it. Deep creases zigzagged the back of my neck, like cracked mud in the summer sun. I run my fingertips over the wrinkles and recalled how Katheryn used to massage my back and shoulders after a hard day of work, and I knew I had been a better husband and father because of her.

But Katheryn was dead—along with the loved ones from my youth—and I hardly never seen my kids and grandkids. But Chloe had enough to worry about without me nagging her, and since I wasn't having company today, I had all morning to decide whether I wanted to clean up that old hickory or visit my wife's grave.

So I sat and watched the leaves fall in the yard and float across the field—and I realized death come in all colors.

I heard a familiar vehicle and looked down the old, dirt road. The mailman eased around the curve. As he pulled into my drive, dust from his truck thinned and disappeared. Whenever I sat outside, he brung me the mail instead of putting it in the dented, rusted box. He must've thought I was too feeble to climb up and down the steps—but he had no way of knowing I'd never let it come to that.

When he got close, I said, "Munford".

"Mornin', Mr. Hartline!"

"What've I told you about that?"

"Yes sir. The other just don't come natural."

He set one foot on the second step and handed me a couple of envelopes. I dropped them on the table without a glance. Pepper raised his eyes to Munford but remained curled at my side.

"You doin' alright?"

I nodded. "Gettin' by."

Munford scratched his sideburns and looked at the deep-blue sky. A breeze blowed the tree branches, their thinning canopies casting the lean shadows of autumn across fading grass. Gold leaves spun and reflected sunlight as they drifted to the ground. "Shapin' up to be a fine day!"

I heard the hollow sound of dead leaves clattering across the porch floor. "Ain't it, though?"

Acknowledgements:

I want to thank family and friends for support and encouragement. Numerous people read the manuscript, and I appreciate the feedback they provided. Also, a special callout to my literature and writing instructors throughout my school years.

I specifically thank the following folks:

-Breandan Lumpkin (publisher): For taking a chance on an unknown writer (coupled with a poor initial pitch) for Co-Pilot's first work of fiction.

-Matthew Clark (graphic designer): For the most amazing novel cover I have seen. (Please, judge my book by its cover.)

-Ellen Zolkos (editor): For relevant recommendations to improve my novel—and for embracing the southern slang.

-Carol Plum-Ucci (author): For proactively offering to write a review for someone she had never met, just because she wanted to support an unpublished writer. Much appreciated.

About the Author:

Mark grew up in northeast Alabama on Puddin' Ridge. After earning an M.A. in English from The University of Tennessee at Chattanooga, he lived in Colorado for several years, then returned home in 2016. For personal interests, he enjoys reading, creative writing, breweries, college football, scuba diving, rock climbing, snow skiing, trout fishing, and— foremost—trail running. He has instructed writing and literature courses for a handful of colleges.

Laying Autumn's Dust is his debut novel.

To learn more about the author, visit MarkLBrooks.com.